THE SEEDS OF AMARANTH

BOOK TWO

REACTIVATING THE CODES

Heather Charnley

Seeds of Amaranth
Reactivating the Codes

Copyright
© Heather Charnley
Purple Spirit
Press 2016
ISBN 978-1-907042-25-6

This book is dedicated to those who believe in the constructive freedom of spiritual understanding and expression to contribute to our world.

Book cover photography and design
Copyright © Sam L. Rollinson 2016

HEATHERS FOREWORD
Synopsis of Book 2 - Reactivating the Codes

The weather is improving and springtime returns, as the alabaster jar has been returned to the Garden of Eden, and the closed vortices to stop renegades are reopened.

The Summer Islands off the coast of Atlantis near Chalidocea is a visitor attraction and Maraya and Costillo decide to go. On swimming round the central island of Elaharia, Maraya disappears. Costillo alerts the mainland temples, they research temple records to find she disappeared via a vortex.

Hudlath, another high priest of the mountain temple goes in search of her. He follows the vortex back in time, travelling several thousand years to when the Summer Islands were part of the northern continent. He doesn't find Maraya so returns.

Meanwhile, Alyssia, one of the Oswestry group, went to Old Oswestry hill fort and sees a vision of Maraya with dolphins, and a mass of coded symbols stream into her. She returns to Plas Myrddin, unable to deal with the codes, as they are continually visible to her. Hudlath takes her to Anchorin's temple; and they download the codes, thus allowing Alyssia to recuperate.

Sarah finds a charming cottage to buy, and on viewing it they find a curious well with codes painted on an inserted ceramic bowl. She dreams of visiting the well, and it appears to her in a shamanic manner.

Sarah and Karin also return to Atlantis to trace the origins of the vortex, and they discover it is a light year portal created by the Pleiadeans, and the high priest Galaron who is closely related to them, knows how to travel along it. He discovers the vortex has taken Maraya towards the Pleiades, then taken by beings who don't work for the Council of Twelve.

Hudlath, Costillo, the Oswestry group, and friends of Jadeir the elf go to rescue Maraya. They travel on the Council of Twelve's spaceship from the earlier time period, and use the Atlantean codes to re-energise the star-way to the destination planet, Pelucia, to clear its darkened atmosphere and transform it to its former bright and energetic state. With that in place, it is relatively easy to rescue Maraya; seal off Pelucia, while ensuring the star-ways of the universe are well upgraded and energised. Their return flight sees them land on a planet of crystals, where Maraya is given deep healing.

3

LIST OF PEOPLE

Sarah Blenheim – healer and craftsperson, near Oswestry
Alyssia Lacey – artist from Kendal
Karin Sloane – runs Plas Myrddin, Oswestry
Kenny Kenton – Karin's partner, runs Plas Myrddin
Maraya – one of Moroccan group, who now lives on Atlantis
Costillo – doorkeeper of Moroccan group, lives on Atlantis
Sagario – crystal holder, Moroccan group, lives on Atlantis
Danuel – crystal holder, Moroccan group, lives on Atlantis
Bertha – shop assistant, Plas Myrddin
Sandra – therapist, Plas Myrddin
Geraldine – healer and friend of Sarah
Annie – neighbour to Sarah's new house
Jaysangar – passenger on spaceship going to Pylon of Phairos
Alendrin & Miara – Sarah's well elementals

Anchorin – high priest in Atlantis – 12,000 BC
Uyindin – priest in Anchorin's temple
Gandan – priest in Anchorin's temple
Jadeir – elf, who comes to help the Oswestry group
Pireus, Ganem, Calani and Derien –Jadeir's Atlantean elf friends
Hudlath – high priest from a time period 200 years after Anchorin
Chanubim – priest of Chalidocea, Anchorin's time
Angarin – priest of Chalidocea, Anchorin's time
Getherin – priest of Chalidocea, Anchorin's time
Tiranuth – priest of Chalidocea, Anchorin's time
Zalarin – high priest at sea temple, Anchorin's contemporary
Frejan – priest in Zalarin's temple
Andal – priest in Zalarin's temple
Engalin – high priest before Zalarin
Melcharin – high priest on Elaharia in 20,400 BC
Gadar – priest from Melcharin's temple
Keirion – high priest at sea temple in 23,000 BC
Galaron – high priest from Lemuria and Elaharia, various times
Aihalaran – high priest from northern island of Atlantis
Sanjeron – high priest from northern island of Atlantis

The Council of Twelve–12,000 BC	The Council of Twelve – 20,400 BC
Zanadar –Cassiopeia	**Zarhavar** – Cassiopeia
Aurion –Sirius	**Aurial** - Sirius
Salaron –the Pleiades	**Salodan** – the Pleiades
Gelsior–Pollux	**Sirankal**-Andromeda
Siral–Andromeda	**Selahon**-Pleiadean crew-member

Caelina and Alaya – Taurus constellation
Elana, Elan and Eloya – fairies at Elaharia

Garalph, Leannah, Gadair & Kavanos – elementals from Pistyl Rhaeadr

Eldina – healer from the planet Pharon, Pylon of Phairos

CONTENTS

Heather's foreword   **P3**

List of people in the book   **P4**

Chapter 1 – New Beginnings   **P7**

Chapter 2 – The Sea Temple & the Summer Islands

                                                         P25

Chapter 3 – Hudlath Time Travels to the North Island

                                                         P40

Chapter 4 – The Discovery   **P55**

Chapter 5 – Summoned to the Temple   **P66**

Chapter 6 –Ty Bach & the Atlantean Vortex   **P77**

Chapter 7 – Voyage Across the Galaxy   **P99**

Chapter 8 –Healing the Pelucian Star-Way   **P115**

Chapter 9 –The Crystalline Planet of Healing   **P133**

Chapter 10 –The Promise in the Well   **P152**

An Overall View of the Trilogy   **P163**

Reactivating the Codes

Chapter 1 – New Beginnings in Chalidocea

Maraya and Costillo were the first two of the Moroccan group to leave Anchorin's beautiful mountain temple. They smiled radiantly to Sagario and Danuel, and then waved to the others as they began walking down the path.

As with all people in Atlantis in the most peaceful eras, the people all communicated telepathically, and the inhabitants' clairsentient gifts were enhanced by visits to their local temples. The Moroccan group had all visited the temples as well.

"I'm so looking forward to being in our new home together Costillo!" said Maraya, her dark features lit up readily, and she looked so much happier than she had done for a long time, "I never thought it would turn out like this!"

"I know Maraya," replied Costillo, equally radiant, "once the renegades took me through the vortex onto Colony Y, I thought I'd never see you or anyone I knew again," and he shrugged.

"You know, Anchorin promised that we should be entering springtime again right now," remarked Maraya.

"Yes indeed," replied Costillo, "ever since he returned the alabaster pot of essence to the Garden of Eden, I've sensed the stirrings of the earth revitalising itself."

"I do hope we will really see some evidence of spring as we descend out of this mist," smiled Maraya, and Costillo smiled back. They both continued arm in arm.

Anchorin, Danuel and Sagario were walking to Anchorin's office, which was half way down the corridor.

"I'm sure a nice cottage dwelling will be made available for you both very soon, I'll just contact the Chalidocean temple of healing, as they have the tally," said Anchorin.

He turned to look directly at the two of them. He was an impressive figure, and taller than most. His violet eyes looked intently, and his long face was framed by long grey hair. Anchorin touched a large quartz crystal, focussing on it a moment. The face of a priest hovered around the crystal.

"Ah! Hello Tiranuth, do you know when that other dwelling will be ready for these two young men who wish to share one," asked Anchorin.

"Almost ready Anchorin, maybe another day or two, then we can have the blessing ceremony when they come," answered Tiranuth, "could I ask if they are single or expecting to join hands with life partners?"

"No life partners involved," replied Anchorin, "yet!"

He gave Sagario and Danuel a quizzical look as he said this and they both smiled. They all said goodbye to Tiranuth and made their way out of the office.

"Can we do some more jobs around here to pass the time Anchorin?" asked Sagario.

"Yes, yes, certainly my boy!" remarked Anchorin, "I expect you both feel it too; I mean the lack of contact with the other time periods. Our friends in Oswestry in the 21st century and my old friend Hudlath from 200 years ahead, and even the Council of Twelve spaceship with Melkior, Zanadar, Aurion and the group cannot communicate very easily. I know it is a symptom of the time portal's closure and legend has it that they may have to remain sealed for many hundreds of years, but there are ways to open them again sooner, I'm sure of that! The beings in the Garden of Eden told me that it was possible."

"How can they be re-opened Anchorin?" asked Danuel.

"It won't happen until the essence catalyses Atlantis into a late spring," explained Anchorin, "but we must all help in that by visualising nature's return to what it was like. Don't worry! We have the added advantage of our crystals and the three caskets. The monks are already doing their best as often as they can each day," he said reassuringly, seeing their concerned faces, "come and join us, but before we go through to our crystal meditation room, let's contact Maraya and Costillo, so they can link in with us too."

Anchorin brought out a crystal from within one of his waist pouches and focused on it. Maraya's face appeared in front of the crystal, and the two men gathered around Anchorin, watching.

"Maraya! Costillo!" called Anchorin, "we are all about to focus on projecting our love, light and visualisation for Atlantis' return to springtime, will you join in?"

"Certainly Anchorin, we'll stop and link in now," replied Maraya.

"Perhaps we should have stayed with you, the visualisation would have been more effective surely with us there too?" questioned Costillo, his face appearing to Anchorin and the others with a pertinent expression.

"No, no! How far down are you? Can you see any scenery yet?" asked Anchorin.

"Yes we can very easily because we are near the bottom," admitted Maraya with a laugh, "the snow has nearly melted away."

"You didn't cheat by using a mountain buggy did you?" said Anchorin with a disapproving look, "any extra energy is vital to restore our world."

"No, we hovered down using our crystals!" responded Costillo.

"Oh good, I'll let you off!" replied Anchorin, "regarding projecting the good energy, it will be an advantage, as an even dispersal of our thought processes makes the healing of Atlantis more efficient, and you'll be able to physically see the results down there more directly than we can from our misty heights!"

Anchorin and the others joined the monks in the crystal meditation room, where the crystals stood on pedestals, which could be moved around to suit the nature of any requirements. In this case, there was a large space in the centre of the room and the pedestals were arranged in a circle around with crystals pointing outwards. Everyone quietly focused on projecting the light, love and images of nature's growth outwards to the trees, grass and shrubs across the country, especially to the earth, and all the seeds and potential plants there.

Sagario and Danuel could see white light projecting outwards in all directions, together with a deep pink and emerald green colour.

Meanwhile, Maraya and Costillo projected out to the countryside intently, and could also see sparkling white light, with the deep pink and emerald green colours radiating out and also down into the earth. They could see the ground shimmering as more light from all the people of Atlantis focused on projecting it out. The main sources of light energy came from the temples, and they could both see it growing increasingly stronger.

Their focus sent energy to the beautiful waterfall at the base of the mountain, where Sarah of the Oswestry group had felt she had lived beside as a seer in a previous lifetime.

Maraya and Costillo stopped concentrating and looked at each other.

"I think they've stopped sending for the moment," remarked Maraya.

"Yes, I believe so," replied Costillo, "I'm sure it will work with all this energy around now, I've got a good feeling about it," and he smiled happily at Maraya.

"Look, Costillo, over there!" said Maraya suddenly, "it's the energy, it's doing something!"

"It certainly is," replied Costillo, having turned to look, "I think it's travelling along a ley line from the waterfall."

"Yes, and more energy elsewhere is beginning to do the same," said Maraya, "It's very encouraging since it is only a matter of days since we all returned from the last days of Atlantis, and then Anchorin returned the alabaster pot through that blizzard, to the Garden."

"Absolutely, I'm sure that Anchorin is right," agreed Costillo, "after all, it's all about intending things to develop to their best advantage, and they do it all the time here!"

"It's wonderful to be able to stay here," exclaimed Maraya and she flung her arms around Costillo, and they danced around together for a moment, and then they continued their journey towards the capital city of Chalidocea.

"Can you see the network of energy streams everywhere now, Maraya?" asked Costillo.

"Yes I can Costillo," she replied, "all the circuitry is becoming very active now, as the earth becomes increasingly more alive, and especially at the pace it does in springtime here. What a beautiful shade of green this energy is, and it is brighter than usual."

"How do you know it's brighter than usual Maraya?" asked Costillo curiously, "it's as if you've lived here before?"

Maraya looked at Costillo directly and he could see something shimmering around her and in her eyes. They had both slowed down and were now standing still, and the entrance gates to Chalidocea were within sight. Costillo could see Maraya's eyes turn violet and her face became very fair, with a mass of flaxen hair cascading over her shoulders, and she was smiling at him.

"Do you not remember when I was the priestess of the sea? You were there too! Remember!" she said.

A feeling of poignancy filtered through Costillo from deep within his heart, yet it didn't made him sad; on the contrary, he began to feel a soulful stirring, and then a faint memory came into his mind, like unearthing something from the archaeological past, he could feel different clothes on himself and a headdress too.

"I was a priest!" he announced, "and we worked together."

He began to smile too, and then the pale face and flaxen hair vanished, and all he could see now were Maraya's brown eyes glistening with tears. They kissed each other and hugged for a while.

"I so wished you would know this! I saw you as I knew you had been, a priest with violet eyes, a tall headdress and a long white gown," said Maraya, "and I knew at that moment you were seeing us both as we were then. I could also feel how moved you were."

"We have known each other a long time, that's for certain my dear," said Costillo. He took Maraya by the shoulders, holding her at arm's length and looking intently at her with a smile.

"Before you came to Morocco, you told me you had lived in Athens, working as a tourist guide, and then you began to give your readings with the tarot, are you sure you are telling me the whole truth, did you really live in Athens?" he asked.

Maraya cast her eyes over to the horizon a moment, watching a winged horse gliding gracefully across some foothills until it disappeared from view.

"Costillo dear," she began, "I didn't tell you the whole truth at the time, as I thought you would have considered me very strange. I did live in Athens for about six months, but before that, I had lived in Atlantis!"

"Ah! The truth at last Maraya!" smiled Costillo, "if only you had told me earlier, you needn't have kept it from me you know!"

Maraya smiled with relief.

"It just seemed easier Costillo," she replied.

"What time period did you come from?" he asked curiously again.

"I came from an earlier time than Anchorin's, before the sea temples had been built and we used natural places that lent themselves to be used as places of worship, and we could more freely feel part of the sea like that, and the dolphins could approach more easily too," she explained.

"Would you ever like to return to that time period? After all, if that's where you came from?" asked Costillo.

"This time period is fine. I like it, and besides, I've begun to know a new group of people now, so it's fine Costillo," and she laughed happily.

"Come on then!" said Costillo, and he put his arm around her and they approached the entrance gates of the city.

"I do like our new cottage!" said Maraya gaily, "it's charming." Maraya and Costillo looked at the exterior. It had been built, like all the other buildings in Atlantis, in red and black stones to a circular design, and with a conical thatched roof.

The local priest had arrived, and he wore the customary band around his forehead, with a crystal at the front, plus a long white cape with gold and deep blue edging, and he greeted them. It was customary for priests to meet the new owners of a dwelling in order to make their acquaintance if they had moved from another town or village, as well as to bless the building.

"Greetings to you both, I am Amarin," he said cordially. He was tall and slim as most Atlanteans were, and though he had deep blue eyes, his hair was darker than most, which pleased Costillo, who had a Mediterranean complexion. "Would you like to see around your cottage first?" he asked.

They went inside as Amarin held open the door, and he took them to the central area.

"This is the meditation area," he said.

There were benches around the perimeter and a small grate where ceremonial fires would be lit or incenses burned, and a small table nearby, and they noticed that it had a stone floor, for safety. They moved back into the first room that they had entered from the front door, which they had noticed was the living room area, and it had seating, cupboards and a circular table.

"The cooking area Is next to the left side, and we have provided work benches and cupboards. The next room beyond is a bedroom," he said, and they both looked approvingly.

They all viewed the rooms on the other side, where there were two more rooms, for sleeping or other uses, and then the priest Amarin said he would give blessings on the house, after he went outside to pick up a container of smouldering logs to bring indoors. He placed it on the grate in the meditation room and proceeded to scatter incense on top, which immediately produced a dramatic mass of smoke. It filled the whole cottage with a strong fragrance, not unlike frankincense, but a bit sweeter. As the blessing came to a close, white light filled the whole cottage and there was a knock on the door.

Maraya was about to say something, when Amarin smiled and put his finger to his lips. She went to the door and opened it. There stood Jadeir the elf and his friends, as well as a group of fairies, gnomes and a unicorn.

Amarin silently beckoned them in, and they all arranged themselves in a circle through all the rooms, while the unicorn stood at the entrance. All the nature spirits concentrated and activated their power of projection and a mass of green light spun round inside the building, and then they linked it to the source of life in the heavens, and deep into the centre of the earth. A chorus of sounds could be heard, which gave the house a pristine energy, and a radiance that would remain while the place was occupied.

Once the ceremony was finished, Maraya and Costillo went to greet their friend Jadeir and the other nature spirits and thanked them.

"Thank you so much for coming over, especially when you're very busy helping the restoration of Atlantis," said Maraya.

"Well, we wanted to see your new home, as well as yourselves in a peaceful abode after our experiences with the renegades," commented Jadeir, "besides, if we happen to be passing by.." he added with a hint.

"Jadeir's quite partial to cheesecake now, after staying with the Oswestry group!" explained Maraya with a chuckle.

"I see!" responded Costillo, "well, I'm sure we can oblige on occasions!"

"I'm so glad," answered Jadeir with a grin, then his expression changed to one of alertness, "we're going to have to return as the energy needs some activating right now, so goodbye and blessings to all!"

Jadeir bowed very low and the other nature spirits also bowed and curtsied.

"After you ladies," he said politely to the fairies, who smiled kindly to Amarin, Maraya and Costillo, and then all said goodbye in unison. Coloured lights danced around them as they moved, and silvery energy began to weave from them, and left shimmering pools of light around the house, growing brighter as they departed, and then all the nature spirits vanished, leaving emerald lights in their wake.

Then the unicorn sent out an effervescent energy from his horn, which came into the house, bringing a pearly light that permeated everywhere, and also gently settled on everyone's heads and shoulders.

"Thank you dear unicorn!" said Maraya and Costillo together.

The unicorn looked at Maraya and Costillo a moment, his eyes glowed radiantly, and they could see an image of the Garden of Eden in them.

He bowed too and said, "that's my pleasure!" and departed silently.

"They don't seem to make any sound when they walk," remarked Costillo.

"That's because their feet don't actually touch the ground," said Amarin, "they just appear to!"

"Your dwelling is well and truly blessed now, Maraya and Costillo!" said Amarin, "a blessing fit for a priest and priestess! Aha! Time to go! I can hear a call from someone of the other side of Chalidocea, goodbye."

"Goodbye and thank you so much Amarin," they replied.

"Let us give thanks to the Great Creator, and also help Anchorin in his endeavour to bring back springtime," said Maraya.

Costillo instantly agreed and they went into the central meditation room and began. Their prayerful energies joined in with many others, streaming out brilliant sparkling light of varying hues, which projected towards the earth, along ley lines and to energy points; bringing that radiance back into the earth. In many places underground the dormant seeds and plants stirred and began their first inklings of movement.

A few days later, Sagario and Danuel had now been granted a home too, and were making their way down the mountain. Once they reached their cottage, Amarin and the retinue duly welcomed them, and performed their house-warming ceremony.

"Maraya, is that you?" asked Sagario, as he had picked up his crystal, which was emitting a flashing white light. An image of Maraya's smiling face appeared.

"Greetings, Sagario and Danuel in your new home!" she replied, and at that point Danuel came over to look. "Costillo sends his greetings too. We are both now working at the temple. Do come over and see if you wish to work there too, though you are welcome to just wander around and see what you'd like to get involved in, as people will show you what to do if you want to, say, try making furniture, homes, or anything else; as Anchorin said, just try it and see how you like it. There's no pressure to work to the degree as in the time period of the Oswestry group."

"Hm, I think I might like to grow plants," said Danuel thoughtfully.

"I still don't know yet what to do," replied Sagario, "I'll experiment!"

"We could show you around the healing temple anyway," said Maraya.

"Yes, let's go Danuel!" replied Sagario enthusiastically.

"Can we come over now, if that's all right?" responded Danuel, leaning towards the crystal, and Maraya agreed that it would.

Danuel and Sagario traversed the roads of Chalidocea, which were arranged in a concentric formation. Their house, and Maraya and Costillo's were both situated near the periphery of the city, and they had to cut across those ring routes to reach the main healing temple, which wasn't difficult as it's orichalcum dome was visible from all areas in Chalidocea.

On entering, they found Maraya waiting there, dressed elegantly in the healing temple clothing, consisting of a long white robe, with a deep blue sash at her waist, and a silver headband with a deep blue crystal in the centre of it. Inside the entrance was a reception area with circular seating around a mass of plants.

"Amaranth plants!" exclaimed Danuel.

The two of them stopped to look at them, for the flowers were beautiful, and they noticed fairies at work, sending sparkling energy to the flowers. Then they noticed the gnomes working on large quartz and amethyst rocks on the far side, imbuing them with green energy.

"Your outfit looks impressive, Maraya," commented Sagario.

They greeted each other cordially, and then Maraya took them to a reception room at the top of the stairs.

"I think it will be worth your while seeing Getheran. He can give you inspiration as to the work options available in Atlantis," said Maraya.

"That sounds very useful, as I haven't decided yet on what to do," replied Sagario.

"Although I would like to work with plants, I would also like to keep an open mind to see what else goes on in Atlantis," responded Danuel happily.

They all proceeded upstairs.

"Where is Costillo?" asked Sagario quickly looking around at the temple interior as they walked, then he gave Maraya a direct look.

"Costillo is busy with the priest, and he intends to specialise in surgery," replied Maraya.

"I'm so pleased," replied Sagario with a delighted chuckle and Danuel cheered.

"Many years ago, he did mention one time, that if he ever had his time again, he would do medical training," remarked Sagario.

"Yes, I knew it was something he always held close to his heart," replied Maraya, "and dreams like that can come true much easier here!"

They all stopped near a door, for Maraya had indicated for them to enter. Once inside, they saw Getherin sitting beside a small table, and he got up on seeing them enter. He was tall and fair-haired with pale blue eyes. His hair came down to his shoulders, and he also wore a white robe and shawl.

"I know I can be of assistance to you both, it is whether you would like it, which is the next question for which I need to know the answer!" he said jovially.

Sagario and Danuel offered their hands, and all four of them sat down in a circle.

"Would you like to talk to me in private or as we are here?" asked Getherin.

"We are quite happy as we are, aren't we Sagario?" asked Danuel, looking at Sagario. Sagario affirmed that he was happy enough.

"Good!" said Getherin; "now tell me, do you have any preferences or inclinations of what you'd like to do?" asked Getherin.

"I don't have anything in mind," replied Sagario, and then he turned to Danuel.

"I would like to work with plants," replied Danuel.

"Well, there are a few options there. You could talk to a few people I know. In the priesthood there are those who know about herbs, and outside, as we say for those who aren't priests or priestesses, you could simply grow fruits and vegetables, or look after the parklands, or all the trees in the

16

city, and tend the gardens of those whose skills lie elsewhere," explained Getherin.

"There are some good options there, and I'm interested in finding out about all the options," said Danuel.

"Now, to Sagario," said Getherin, looking at him closely, "what would really inspire you, are you artistic, or are you systematic?"

"I am quite a systematic person, as I used to work with computers, and I programmed them," replied Sagario, "but I wouldn't mind a change from that!"

"You could work in our research chambers. They sort out and investigate much, such as new ways of healing and uses of crystals, to new ways of governing, and much else," explained Getherin, "does any of that interest you?"

"Yes, I think it does," replied Sagario looking pleased, "I am not sure which facet as yet I would get involved in, but the general themes appeal to me a great deal."

"I shall see who needs help the most. Perhaps you can try it for a few days, and see whether it suits both sides, eh!" said Getherin with a cheerful grin.

The three of them left Getherin and went downstairs, past the reception area to just outside the entrance.

"We'll just await the next step, for the temple to contact us now, Maraya," remarked Sagario, and Danuel murmured agreement.

"They won't take long, and you may even hear by tomorrow morning, my friends," replied Maraya, "I must return now, as I have work to do."

"We'll just explore the area, Maraya," said Danuel.

He and Sagario waved goodbye to Maraya as they walked away. Meanwhile, she went up the steps and returned indoors again. Sagario and Danuel took a good look at the surrounding area by the temple.

"This hexagonal area around the temple is just as impressive as the temple itself," said Sagario.

"Yes, the buildings have some of the features of the temple, haven't they? Look at those dome-like roofs, touches of orichalcum, spire-like finials at various points, and the doorways are like Middle Eastern buildings, with arches at the top. They are a pleasure to look at!" commented Danuel, "oh, look at those plants across the other side, they're amazing! Do you mind if we go and see them, Sagario?" he asked.

"No problem my friend, let's go!" answered Sagario.

They walked across and as they did, they were aware of priests and lay people wandering to and fro, either to the entrance of the temple or to certain buildings around the temple that Sagario and Danuel were looking at.

The plants they came to were growing very tall, and they studied them closely. They exclaimed when a priest appeared from between two of the plants and greeted them cheerfully.

"Welcome!" he said, "is there anything I can do for you my friends? By the way, my name is Chanubim!"

"I am Danuel and this is Sagario," he said, "we have just been talking with Getherin in the temple. I am very interested in plants, and we spotted yours and came to investigate. Please could you tell me what they are?

"They are elixir plants," replied Chanubim, "they are used for…"

"It's all right, we know what they are used for, my friend," replied Danuel, "I asked because I've only seen them growing in pots.

Chanubim looked surprised at being interrupted, and then realised who they were.

"You were part of the group that was rescued from the Colony Y, weren't you," he exclaimed, "well, you'll know how to use these beauties then! As well as the other plants that were relevant. It's a good sign that they are able to grow again after our winter season. These plants were always the first to getting going, though we can grow anything we want inside too, and have had to during that snowy spell."

Chanubim stopped his chatting and looked intently at Danuel.

"My boy, can you project good energy into this plant without forcing your intent on it, but only in a way that enhances its growth? Do it now!" said Chanubim in a gently authorititive way.

Danuel concentrated hard a moment, then tried to relax and allow energy to run through him. Energy began to come from his forehead, and a white beam tinged with green, deep blue and some pink began to emerge. He then projected it to the stem of the elixir plant nearest to him. The plant responded immediately by growing another six inches, and its leaves glowed with a sunny light.

"Well done! I think you will be working with us!" he responded.

Danuel thanked Chanubim and then he and Sagario wandered off.

"I think that fellow knew who we both were from the first moment!" remarked Sagario.

"I'm sure you're right!" laughed Danuel.

"Oh look! There's a hoverbuggy," exclaimed Sagario, "we can get a ride around town."

"Good thinking," replied Danuel, "we can check up on useful supplies."

The buggy duly stopped and they were taken around the streets where the shops were, although the Atlanteans didn't call them shops, they were 'places of exchange or resources'. Sagario and Danuel got off the buggy and wandered down the street, looking at all the merchandise on offer.

"You know, I still find it hard to believe that we can just take what we need without any payment, even though we know that the work we will be doing, will be our way of paying back into the society's system," remarked Sagario.

"I know, but I don't feel I could take anything until we start working, do you?" asked Danuel.

"No, not yet, besides, the priest Amarin kindly left us enough food for a good week or so in the cupboards," replied Sagario.

"The craftwork is exquisite," remarked Danuel, "I think I'd prefer to go now before I get tempted to take something!"

"Yes, we'll return when we've done some work!" Sagario said to a nearby craft maker sitting outside his workshop as many others were doing. The man had beautifully carved tables and ornaments with dolphins, fairies and elves depicted all over them, and were interspersed with amaranth flowers. The stallholder smiled and said to come back whenever they wished.

When they returned home, a message came up on Danuel's crystal, as its glowing signal was detectable from inside a cupboard in the living room.

"It's Getherin!" exclaimed Danuel, and Sagario swiftly came over to view.

"Hello friends," he said, "we have decided very quickly on this occasion, and need Danuel's help in the priesthood in order to grow and work with the plants. Your meeting with Chanubim speeded things up! As for Sagario, would you like to help our governor priests with their archives and systems? You would be sorting out information initially and work towards your chosen field in time."

"Yes, we are very happy with that," said Danuel, who looked at Sagario and he agreed.

19

"When do we start, please?" asked Sagario.

"Is tomorrow too soon, or do you need a little more time to settle in?" he asked.

"Tomorrow is fine, we're looking forward to doing something," replied Sagario.

"Well, come over tomorrow as soon as you are able to, and call upstairs in my room," said Getherin, "here is a list of the other things I do! Just point your crystal at the white and gold box in the living room, and you'll see the information!"

Danuel duly pointed the crystal at the box and sent energy to it. Immediately some sheets came out of it. Getherin smiled at their surprised faces.

"It's like a fax machine!" exclaimed Danuel, "we thought it was a receptacle for holding paper tissues!"

Getherin laughed, "Yes, I do know that your time period has many gadgets that we have, including containers for paper tissues! Though we discarded a number that were unhealthy or unnecessary, once we realised just how carried away we got at one time in our history, and only have things in moderation now."

"Thank you, we'll read that now. Good, there are two copies!" remarked Sagario, "goodbye until tomorrow Getherin!"

"Goodbye boys!" responded Getherin.

He cheerfully waved, and then they sat down to read the details.

"That's interesting! Getherin gives readings for newly-borns to determine where their future lies, and also sees them when they become 'of age' for further talks," commented Danuel.

"Interesting indeed!" replied Sagario, poring over the information, "I'm reading about how the governing priests work, with regard to the administrative side. I'm looking forward to surveying all those disks!"

"Oh yes, disks," said Danuel, "that reminds me about the caskets. I wonder whether we'll ever see the contents of them?"

"I've no idea," replied Sagario, "I did ask Anchorin what would happen to them now, and he said that they would need to stay closed for some time."

"Perhaps until the weather improves," said Danuel, "so that all is stable again, as we knew that they were detectable by various sources when open."

"Yes, maybe if they were opened too soon, the problem of the vortices activating and possibly being accessible to the darker time periods may re-occur before appropriate stabilisation has taken place," said Sagario, "so, the caskets may be helping the climate by staying shut; and because all the contents, including the crystals and disks being together, they may be acting as catalysts."

"It's the appointed hour for sending out healing to the earth, Sagario!" cried Danuel, suddenly remembering.

"Let's go to the meditation chamber then!" replied Sagario eagerly.

They linked to their crystals, and to others who were also sending out thoughts. They asked for the divine source to channel energy via themselves towards the planet and especially Atlantis, for the wintry season had hit Atlantis the worst. Energy swirled around them and soared out of the house, linking with other energy, while some went straight into the ground.

Maraya finished preparing the meal in their kitchen one evening and turned to Costillo, who was reading something at the table.

"That must be the boys coming!" she remarked.

Costillo looked up with that half-surprised look people give when they've been lost in concentration.

"Ah, you're right! I should have heard that pebble being crunched two streets away! You have remarkable hearing Maraya!" teased Costillo.

"I can see them coming clairvoyantly, dear!" laughed Maraya.

"Your skills are better than mine, I still can't do that if I'm concentrating on something else," replied Costillo.

Maraya went to open the door and welcomed Sagario and Danuel, ushering them inside.

"Come in boys!" she said.

"Don't mind if we do!" replied Sagario.

"Honoured to be in such edifying priestly company!" responded Danuel.

Maraya laughed and Costillo ushered them over to sit at the table.

"I'll just dish up," said Maraya, "and Costillo will get the drinks."

"She's at a higher priestly level than me, so I have to take the orders!" winked Costillo.

"How long do you reckon it will take before the continent resumes normality?" asked Sagario, "the priesthood will know more than the general public won't they?"

"That's true, they do," replied Costillo, "I was talking about it to some of the seer priesthood and they were impressed at how quick it has been to recuperate, and definitely due to the caskets being intact, and all back at Anchorin's temple."

"That's what we thought," said Danuel.

"They think it will take a few more weeks and we will have spring to look forward to," replied Maraya happily, "and then we will be nearly back to normal!"

"What about time travel? Will we be able to come and go as we could before?" asked Sagario.

"The priests don't know as yet, because it usually takes so much longer than the springtime's appearance," replied Maraya.

"How many times has this happened before?" asked Danuel curiously.

"It happened once before in Atlantis, during the first civilised period, when the culture declined, and also at the end of the Lemurian period," explained Maraya, "the climate was very bad indeed, but only in those areas where the catastrophes happened."

"You mean the demise and final break up of the continents?" asked Sagario.

"Yes, though I know that such events obviously have a world wide impact, as do the weather patterns themselves, but as far as the eternal winter scene, that tends to be only on the relevant continents. If that continent had slipped under the sea, however, it is that area of the sea which is affected," explained Maraya.

"I'm still not sure why this winter shut down period has lifted away at top speed. Does anyone have a proper explanation for it?" asked Sagario, "I mean, how can a casket make so much difference?"

"It does seem extraordinary, but I've got word recently from Anchorin that all the priests in his mountain temple were guided to put the three caskets in the crystal healing room, and once they were in there, there was a surge of energy that went out from them down into the earth, and it also linked up with the alabaster pot at the Garden of Eden," explained Maraya.

"The caskets must have being working to a degree before they were taken into the crystal healing room, Maraya, in order to do that, surely," commented Costillo, "strange that it wasn't noticed."

"I think they were activated when the alabaster pot was returned. It wasn't noticeable as it happened very gently," replied Maraya.

Danuel's forehead had formed into thoughtful creases, and he sat with his head on his hand, eyes focused on the table.

"Danuel, you look as if your pondering on something, do tell us!" said Costillo.

Danuel looked up suddenly, hardly aware that he was so lost in thought and he smiled.

"Oh yes, I was lost in thought!" and he smiled, "I was thinking about those previous cataclysms, and the correlation between them and the caskets. Had the caskets been missing ever since the beginning of Atlantean culture, or at the end of Lemuria?" he asked.

"That's a good point Danuel!" replied Maraya, "I don't think the priests will know fully until they begin to look inside at the contents, and they can't do that until things are reverted to normal again."

In his office Anchorin peered through his crystal to scry for progress outside. He could clairsentiently see everything stirring, and that spring would come very soon. His face took on a serious air now.

'I do hope that all will be well once the spring arrives, I cannot even contact my friends for their advice,' he thought, as he tried to focus hard on Zanadar's, Aurion's and Melchior's faces, but to no avail, nothing came through. 'What will really happen when the portals open again? Perhaps I should warn everyone in Atlantis to be observant. I really should have asked the guardian beings of the alabaster pot, Anui, Deanu and Giana, in the Garden of Eden when I was there.'

Anchorin tried to link with them. He couldn't see any of them at all, but heard some voices.

"I am speaking to someone from the Garden of Eden aren't I?" he asked.

The unmistakeable sound of several voices in unison came more clearly, "Yes, it is the Sentinel. Our group are here and know you are concerned about something. It is the portals' opening, that is it! As far as we know, with the caskets all intact, there shouldn't be too much of a problem, and there hopefully won't be one with the renegades as far as we can see."

"I certainly hope not," responded Anchorin, "but do you know what happened to the renegades once all the portals closed?"

"Yes, they were all strangely drawn away into the end times, and from there, they were sucked into the main vortex and transported in an instant to their planet, and the colonies before it closed, as it was planned to happen," said the Sentinel.

"Ah good! Glad it was as planned!" Well, I feel a little happier knowing that. I should have asked you when I returned the alabaster pot, but I didn't, as I thought it would be too soon to know the final outcome of what happened, and I wasn't used to such terrible weather!" Anchorin replied.

"Yes it was too soon, because of the delayed effect of the various facets along the time span, the latter days at the end of Atlantis being the last to close, and the last few hundred years always takes longer," answered the Sentinel.

"Would you know when I can contact the Council of Twelve?" asked Anchorin.

"Once the last frosts have gone I'm sure, which could only be in a few more day's time," said the Sentinel.

Chapter 2 – The Sea Temple and the Summer Islands

The joyful face of Zanadar came through to Anchorin. His red skin looked positively sunny, with a warm glow around him. Anchorin could see the thought form of him that Zanadar himself had sent, and it had zoomed into his office and hung there. When Anchorin apprehended its arrival from another part of the temple, he almost ran through it to obtain his crystal in the office.

He put his head around the office door, "It's Zanadar!" he exclaimed to his colleagues, "he's coming through at last!"

They all smiled happily and then began to clap their hands, laugh and show various ways of expressing their joy. Anchorin had emerged from his office. He looked at them and chuckled at their excitement. Once returned to his office he saw the thought form again.

"Hello Zanadar!" he said to the smiling thought form, "I'm glad your creator of the same name can reach us again!"

It waved and said, "contact me," and then faded away.

"Zanadar, welcome to our planet again!" said Anchorin excitedly, via his activated crystal.

Zanadar's face hovered over the crystal, smiling.

"Welcome back to the Universe Anchorin!" he replied, "were there some questions needing answers? We could just about see you, and if not on occasions, sense you had concerns, but of course couldn't find out much more."

"I had been concerned about the portals when they open up, as to what to expect at that moment when they do. I hope no more renegades, or side effects of one sort or another, I don't know! Do you?" asked Anchorin.

"We have been studying and discussing this matter carefully and concluded that the portals all over Atlantis are now re-awakening and opening. Most will be safe enough, but some may be linked to unknown places, especially some new portals, which have begun to open now.

"You see, although you are experiencing a golden age there, because the caskets had disappeared and are now returned intact, their influence and completeness has caused these new portals to open in accordance with the time period and places in the universe they were originally linked with when they were last intact!" explained Zanadar.

"Ah, I see what you mean," responded Anchorin, "we shall have to make a note of these new portals when we find them, and see how they operate." A glimmer of concern crossed Anchorin's face, "I hope there will be no surprises in store as a result."

"Yes, that's right," replied Zanadar, "whether they are inactive when someone accesses them, or otherwise, and people are whisked off somewhere. I hope we can discover them first!"

"This will need some monitoring," replied Anchorin, "the portals will all have to be recorded again, and checked over continuously as some were known in the past to be very irregular and so were avoided or closed. I shall have to gather my resources on those old techniques of working with portals, for these new ones may be Lemurian in origin. I shall contact the Chalidocean temple to help us survey the land clairsentiently as it will be safer."

Anchorin looked thoughtful a moment, and then looked at Zanadar again.

"Do you have any relevant information to hand, my friend?" he asked.

"Certainly I do!" replied Zanadar, "a list of references to check in your main library in the intergalactic and time periods sections, and this was stored in our files."

With a sudden flash of light, some information came out of Anchorin's white box.

"You don't have to be so dramatic!" said Anchorin; "I nearly got a burn mark on my robe! Not unlike a certain elf who did fire-cracking tricks beside my old friend Hudlath on Colony Y!"

"Well, you wanted the information quickly, there it is!" teased Zanadar, still smiling, which provoked a wry expression from Anchorin.

"Thank you very much!" he replied, with a twinkle in his eyes.

Zanadar's face faded and Anchorin reached for the information.

'I'll inform the temple at Chalidocea once I've gone through this,' he thought, and he sat and read it in the office.

It was an exceptionally warm day, and all the spring growth was becoming well established. It was the day of rest for Maraya and Costillo, for the temples planned people's work schedules very considerately, so that couples could have some of their time off together.

"Are you ready Costillo?" asked Maraya.

"Nearly!" came a voice from the bedroom on the left side of the house.

Costillo emerged a few moments later with his bag and headed for the door, and they both exited together.

"I hope we can get a hoverbuggy easily," commented Costillo.

"Let's go past the temple and get onto Summer Islands Way, and then I'm sure we'll find masses of them," suggested Maraya.

"I hope they'll want to go all the way there too!" said Costillo.

"I've brought some of the small cakes I made last night, perhaps one or two will inspire the buggy driver!" responded Maraya.

"You think of everything, Maraya!" he replied, and laughed.

They found one of many hoverbuggies on Summer Island Way and set off.

Sagario and Danuel were at the main temple, becoming acquainted with their chosen vocations. Danuel was in Chanubim's garden helping to plant new herb stocks, while Sagario was sifting through some information for a document required for the priests in his department. He took the relevant document through to the priest.

"Thank you Sagario, this will acquaint you with our extensive archives!" said Angarin, "can you sort out this pile here, my boy?"

"I am searching for information on ancient healing methods, and I know that there are records on it, which are exceedingly old indeed, and known to be kept somewhere in these archives. It was brought to our awareness by one of the healer priests, who reminded me of an ancient legend which went like this. 'In the fall of the year, six crystals tell of the arch six, their sacred secrets hold, and are unforetold. Their plans awry, but the knowledge used is destiny.' This is the full version of the legendary lines, and was usually reduced to 'Six crystals of arch six, their knowledge used is destiny.' So, it seems that something is at large, which will be useful. Let's keep searching!"

Angarin gave a thoughtful look and then swiftly returned to his place, and continued searching through his collection of information.

"But the fall of the year surely means autumn, when the leaves fall, Angarin," said Sagario.

"Yes indeed! There is nothing exceptional about autumn, but in this case, we've just experienced an artificial winter. Yes

Sagario, that is it, thank you my boy. It means now!" replied Angarin.

"The rest of the lines certainly need some thought," responded Sagario, "I wonder why 'unforetold'?"

"It certainly does!" said Angarin, "but I'm sure we'll discover the meaning in due course. I'm beginning to feel increasingly, that it is exceedingly important."

They continued to search, and Angarin beckoned other priests over to help too.

"Angarin, if it means this specific time, what if unexpected things have to happen in order to uncover that information?" suggested Sagario.

Angarin looked at Sagario curiously, "you mean with the land and portals re-awakening?"

"Yes, it may bring fresh perspectives, and something new that wasn't apparent before," suggested Sagario.

"Interesting idea, thank you. We must all keep alert as to the true meaning of this phrase. It's like a half-told prophecy," answered Angarin.

Maraya and Costillo sat in the back of the hoverbuggy looking over towards the area of coast they were heading towards. The sun was behind them and it highlighted the profiles of the Summer Islands, which were just a mile or two away from the coast.

"Maraya, do you know anything about those islands?" asked Costillo.

"Yes Costillo, they are reputed to be the last remnants of the old continent. That is, the part that perished and disappeared into the sea many centuries ago," she explained.

"Really! You mean Lemuria?" he exclaimed and looked at Maraya intensely as if searching her soul for an answer to an unknown question.

Maraya smiled, "no Costillo, still Atlantean, and that's where we're going. It will be a lovely voyage, and I think one of the priests may take us out, or at least they will lend us their sea vessel."

"How often have you been, and how long will it take to reach the island?" he asked.

"I've been quite a few times Costillo, but years ago. It will take less than an hour, so we'll have plenty of time there!" said Maraya happily, and they smiled at each other.

The hoverbuggy came to a slight promontory and indicated that this was as far as he could go. Maraya and Costillo thanked him and then walked off down a rocky track, which ran from the promontory down to the beach.

"What's that sound?" asked Costillo, listening hard, as there were murmuring sounds, followed by the unmistakeable sound of a bell.

"It's the sea temple prayers coming to an end, Costillo!" replied Maraya.

They walked over another raised area of rocks on the beach, and Costillo stopped in his tracks, amazed at the sight. There, ahead of them was the circular sea temple, built on top of the rocks, where there was a natural cove. The building straddled the cove, so that the water was inside the temple, essential for their ceremonies. A priest noticed them coming and wandered over to talk to them.

"We would like to go and visit the Summer Islands, can we take a sea vessel there?" asked Maraya.

"I will ask the high priest, Zalarin," he said, and he disappeared inside the temple.

Shortly afterwards, Zalarin the high priest emerged, dressed in white, with a white headband, complete with crystal and a golden sash round his waist. Maraya and Costillo just had their brooches on to denote their priestly rank, since they were casually dressed for the occasion.

"I'm Zalarin," he said looking at them closely, "and you are Maraya and Costillo. I can show you how to operate the boat my friends. If you get into difficulty, just use your crystal to contact us, I presume you brought one?"

"Yes, we brought my crystal," answered Maraya.

"Come, the vessel is down by the edge of the cove, where there's a tiny inlet," explained Zalarin politely, and he led them to the place.

They duly arrived at the boat, which was securely tucked into the inlet. Zalarin turned to face Maraya and Costillo.

"I know you both. Maraya is a high-ranking priestess in the main temple in Chalidocea, and Costillo is a student priest studying surgery. You are both married and were involved in the Colony Y expedition," he said, looking at them directly, "I am not being nosy. We have to ensure safety ensues, and always do this before anyone uses our boats, also so we know who to contact in an emergency."

"Very sensible and only to be expected," replied Maraya, "it is Costillo who isn't acquainted with our customs."

"Are you visiting all the Summer Islands, and how long will you be? We do like to know some rough details, just in case," said Zalarin.

"I suppose we'll be about four hours at the most," answered Maraya, "we're visiting Elaharia to see the sea temple. I have visited the island two or three times before, but some time ago."

Zalarin looked alertly at them.

"It interests people as they always have good experiences there. I don't recall seeing you before; it must have been Engalin the high priest who saw you before. If you do get into any kind of difficulty, just use your crystal. Very good. Farewell!"

Before Zalarin left, he pointed to an aperture by the engine where they were to place the sea temple crystal inside, with the point facing the engine connector. He gave them the crystal and left.

Costillo placed the crystal in the slot, pulled a lever to reverse slowly, and the vessel reversed out of the inlet. Maraya adjusted the rudder lever so that the vessel turned around gently to make the prow point towards the open sea. Then they sailed off, swiftly gathering speed. The boat sent out an echoing tone to warn the dolphins and other sea life nearby that they were travelling quite fast.

"Oh look! how lovely!" smiled Maraya.

A school of dolphins had leapt out of the water one by one, arcing gracefully; they swam alongside the boat.

"They are the sea temple dolphins!" exclaimed Maraya.

"Really," responded Costillo, and he looked at them intently, "I somehow feel that they want to communicate with us!"

"So do I, when we get to Elaharia," replied Maraya.

Many of the islands had near vertical cliffs, which rose straight out of the water for about 1,000 feet, up to the craggy mountains above. They had sharp edged arêtes, so they were totally unapproachable. The vessel rounded one of the cliff-faced islands to find that all the rocky islands were, in fact, arranged in a circular formation, and in the centre lay another larger island, which was a completely different shape. It had a natural cove, but some of the rocks around the cove, Costillo noticed, had been carved to form steps up to the higher ground.

"This looks more promising," said Costillo.

Maraya smiled and said, "yes, you've guessed it, this is Elaharia."

They approached the shore and secured the vessel, before walking up the beach and clambering up the stone carved steps.

"Where is the sea temple?" asked Costillo, "since you've been here before."

Maraya smiled, "it's further on, but why don't we just explore the island as it's only small. As it was a while ago when I last came, I can't remember all the details, so it would be nice just to look at everything and take our time."

They wandered around to the eastern side of the island, with the warm sun on their backs. Central to the island was a tall, craggy area of rock, with a route covered in vegetation that wound around to the top of it. A group of fairies came over from the side of this promontory and speeded over to Maraya and Costillo.

"Welcome to Elaharia my friends, can we help you?" asked one, "my name is Elana," and my companions are Elan and Eloya."

"My name is Maraya and this is Costillo, my friends," she responded, and they both happily greeted the fairies.

"Elana, is the sea temple just as it was?" asked Maraya, "nothing has changed on the island has it?"

"Nothing at all, Maraya," replied Elana, "the sea temple is still over there in the far cove, it hasn't moved since you were last here!" She pointed northwards and began to laugh.

"We're going to visit it, do you wish to join us for a while?" asked Maraya.

Maraya, Costillo and the fairies continued along the edge of the coastline. There was no path, and as the spring growth had not got too high yet, they were able to progress without any difficulty. The edge of the coast was still higher than the sea level, with a cliff edge in places as high as six feet. To their surprise, once over a rise in the ground, the ground began sloping downwards towards another cove with a sandy shoreline.

"There it is! The sea temple area is by the cove's inlet, don't you remember now?" said Elana, "we have work to do now, but we'll hopefully see you later!"

"Goodbye and thank you," said Maraya and Costillo together.

"Let's go!" said Maraya eagerly.

"Look, there's the dolphins again!" said Costillo, and they looked at each other happily, and proceeded.

Once at the head of the cove, they saw some slabs of rock with walls surrounding the area.

"I feel that they held ceremonies on more than one level here, and also depending on whether they wanted to totally immerse themselves underwater and conduct ceremonies there, either for the whole ceremony or part of it. People learnt how to hold their breath for quite a long time in those days, and the priesthood were trained to do this," commented Maraya.

"Do you want to go into the water Maraya, and communicate fully with the dolphins?" asked Costillo.

"Yes, it would be good," she replied, "would you like to join me?"

"I'm a good swimmer, but don't think I could hold my breath for a whole ceremony, not even past the first stages!" he said.

"Let's just go and see the dolphins and then come out and meditate on what the ceremonies were like," said Maraya.

"Why not meditate first, and then we're more prepared," answered Costillo.

"Ok, your choice!" smiled Maraya.

They sat still on a ledge near the paving stones around the sea temple area. Maraya could see the area vibrantly alive with activity. She could see images of many priests gathering here, greeting the sun, and then the sea life. She could see them stripping off their robes, and underneath they wore short tunic-like under garments. They waded into the sea, and dived below the surface to commune with the dolphins, who offered much inspiration. It seemed to her that the dolphins were part of the priesthood, and elders would go and talk to the dolphins regularly to exchange ideas, obtain advice on how to conduct their affairs, and also find inspiring information they could pass on to the populace. They finished meditating and Maraya told Costillo what she saw.

"I saw much the same Maraya, but the interesting thing was that I saw us both swimming out there!" commented Costillo.

Maraya smiled, "did you see the colour of my hair?"

Costillo thought a moment, "it was blond," and his face expressed realisation, "that must have been the time we were priest and priestess together.

Maraya nodded, "and we lived here!"

"Why did you want us to come here really?" asked Costillo, "not just to reminisce surely!"

"No, Costillo dear, I just had a hunch that I would learn more about being a priestess by coming here," she replied, "and it sometimes takes several trips in order to know anything of the ancient ways."

"Ok then, let's get changed and go and say hello to the dolphins!" said Costillo.

They put on their swimwear now used in Atlantis, which was a thin, filmy, yet opaque material fashioned into a bodysuit with trousers and a wraparound tie at the waist. The water wasn't as cool as it could have been because the waters warmed up easier around Elaharia, for the land underwater was comparatively shallow, and only about four or five fathoms at the most. Once immersed, two of the dolphins swam over. Maraya and Costillo swam up to them and touched the dolphins' heads, and looked into their eyes. A stream of information came into their minds with that.

"We link to you today, for we come from the Pleiades and intend that our lives are ensured to be worthy, as we hold the key to spiritual success on earth. Look into our eyes and our minds will transmit that through you, and then the information stored in your minds will reveal itself in time. We have given you both the same information."

Costillo and Maraya saw a brightness in the dolphins' eyes as the information passed to them. Once it stopped, Maraya and Costillo smiled at each other.

"I feel we ought to swim around with the dolphins to conclude this moment. I can't say why, but feel it's necessary," explained Maraya.

"That is fair enough, let's go swimming with them," replied Costillo.

They both duck dived below the water's surface and followed the dolphins. They soon found that the dolphins paired off with them, so Maraya went with one and Costillo went with the other. The dolphins began circling the island, Maraya and her dolphin went clockwise, and Costillo and his dolphin went anticlockwise.

Costillo expected to see Maraya and her dolphin half way around the island at the south-western area, but he couldn't see them. He returned to the sea temple having swum completely around the island, sometimes underwater and sometimes on the surface. Maraya wasn't there and so they waited a few minutes. He looked at the dolphin with concern and cried, "where can she be?"

The dolphin looked at him intently, trying to reassure Costillo, but he could see that the dolphin was a bit concerned too. Just then, Maraya's dolphin returned, chattering edgily, and Costillo looked intently at the dolphin and picked up the feeling implied that she had vanished. He also got the impression that they ought to leave and report this to the head priest Zalarin, at the sea temple on the mainland, for he would be able to interpret the dolphin's message more effectively. Costillo reluctantly got changed and set off in the vessel as swiftly as he could, returning to the sea temple on the shore.

Zalarin pondered seriously when Costillo recounted every detail of the ceremony, and their pairing with the dolphins.

"I shall have to warn people not to go to the island until we know what is going on. The fact that you chose to go around anticlockwise meant that you were safe, for clockwise movement activates things, but we shall start researching the cause of her disappearance as soon as possible," he said to Costillo.

"Now, my friends," what are your stories?" he said to the dolphins.

Maraya's dolphin chattered and then looked at Zalarin closely.

"He said that he was swimming close to Maraya, and when they were on the south-western side, both the dolphin and Maraya felt a very strong tingling sensation. The dolphin instinctively wheeled around and swam off, but Maraya wasn't so quick, and she cried out that she was being pulled somewhere, and she could see stars coming towards her. The dolphin tried to nudge her away from that place, but then she disappeared.

"It's got to be a portal there," cried Costillo, "but where does it go? Didn't you know about this one?"

"I'm sorry, I didn't, Costillo, for nothing like this has been apparent before," said Zalarin. "It must be this transition period Atlantis has gone through, that has opened it up. I'll look up the records, I'm sure something about it must be in there, about the ancient lands. Come, follow me!"

Costillo glanced at the dolphins who had their heads turned on one side, with concerned expressions in their eyes. He managed to smile to them, and then followed Zalarin to his records office.

"We may have what we're looking for in this section," he said. He wandered to a walk-in room, lined with files, boxes of crystals and disks.

"Should we contact Anchorin, maybe he would know something," suggested Costillo.

"He would only say that we have the records, so we'll just press on, but once we've done what we can here, I'll report to Anchorin and the Chalidocean temple."

"I could contact them myself, as I have my crystal with me," responded Costillo.

"Please do, please do, sorry I should have suggested that, but you may now be aware, I'm concentrating hard on all these crystals at this moment, to ask them to awaken and bring themselves to my notice, or else it would take weeks to get through them all individually," replied Zalarin.

"I understand Zalarin, I'll contact them," said Costillo.

He wandered out of the walk-in room and duly left word with the two temples.

"I've discovered a handful of possibilities," said Zalarin.

He returned to the main records office room holding a tray of five large old quartz crystals on it, three disks and pile of worn files.

"I'll ask some of the priests to help us out," he said.

He sounded a note with a summoning bell. Several priests came through to where Zalarin and Costillo were standing.

I've summoned you because we have an emergency. Maraya the priestess has vanished off the coast of Elaharia," he said.

The priests gave soft cries of surprise and concern; then Zalarin continued, "can you all help by scrying these crystals while Costillo and I look at the disks, and we have some old files too, the language may be a bit difficult to decipher, but we can all work together on that."

Zalarin proffered the crystals for the priests, and then Costillo and he selected a disk each, and placed it on an activating machine. It had a crystal under a small round revolving table, which reminded Costillo of a modern day CD player.

It also span round once the disk was clipped into place, and a bright light shone onto it like a laser, pinpointing the relevant place for retrieving information. The information observed came up on a monitor just above the disk machine, which was constructed of various materials, and coated with various metals including the red tinged orichalcum.

"I've found something!" cried a priest, and he rushed over to Zalarin and Costillo.

"It's ancient language, so I cannot decipher it well, but I think it says this. 'Out of the grandness, a line of light will face those who know.' Maybe it's not much, but it just stood out for me," said the priest.

"Yes, it's interesting," said Zalarin thoughtfully, as if answering Costillo's inquisitive look, he continued, "the grandness is the ancient word for spirit or the heavens, and those who know are the priests and priestesses."

"How is that specifically connected to Elaharia?" asked Costillo.

"It was under a section on portals in ancient times, perhaps it may be relevant, somehow?" suggested the priest, "I will keep looking."

"Good fellow, Frejan, everything is a sign towards what we seek," said Zalarin encouragingly.

On Costillo's screen, an image of some mountains in a circular formation came up, and he gave a shout, which brought everyone rushing over.

"Look everyone! This is the Summer Islands as they were before the submergence of the lands, don't you think?" cried Costillo.

"Well spotted, my lad!" answered Zalarin, "it is indeed."

The priests went back to their places and continued searching.

"Could you all look for maps of the area, or anything else on the ancient languages," said Zalarin.

Costillo continued to study the map of the Summer Islands, where Maraya disappeared. Then three of the priests started talking together, and then they came over to Zalarin and Costillo again, and one of them spoke.

"Zalarin, the three of us have decided that we each have found some kind of language, for our information is similar in style, yet we are unable to decipher it. Would you like to see it?" asked Andal.

"I most certainly would, Andal. Just put them down by Costillo's machine as his has both vision and sound. We might be able to get some of it to sound out if we are lucky," responded Zalarin, "and also see if the language converter will work with it."

Costillo was still looking closely at the image of the Summer Islands region of Old Atlantis, and he enlarged the image and zoomed in.

"I was trying to see if anything would come to light about the vortex on this map, perhaps a mark or indication, but there's nothing to see," said Costillo with a resigned tone.

"Try this crystal that Andal brought, my friend," said Zalarin, "here! I'll put it into the machine."

He turned a knob at the front and a tray sprang outwards, and he placed the crystal in, point facing inwards, and then shut it again.

The face of a priest appeared on the screen, and he was dressed very plainly in natural coloured clothing, as if the community had woven such garments themselves. The language was unintelligible but Zalarin was now searching for translation options.

"That may do it," commented Zalarin. His studious looking face was framed by long grey hair, and he wore a sapphire on the usual headband at his forehead. "I've just found out that the translation converter only goes back to the first priest on our section of Atlantis, and not to those on the submerged land. That man you see now is Aihalaran. We could really do with knowing the language from Sanjeron's time. He was one of the last good high priests on the island, when the civilisation had already begun to deteriorate, and Aihalaran was his contemporary."

"I'd like to ask many more questions Zalarin, but we must concentrate on this job in hand," responded Costillo.

"We need a translator crystal at this minute!" announced Zalarin, first talking to Costillo and then over to the other priests.

The priests brought the box of crystals over and Zalarin arranged them around the machine, testing each one by focusing his attention on each. As he did so, a beam of white light projected from his forehead to the crystal in question, and it glowed. The crystal that glowed pale blue was the one Zalarin chose; the others had been dark blue, golden yellow and pink. The crystal with the pale blue light was duly patted in a friendly manner by Zalarin and placed as close to the other crystal inside the machine as possible.

"I've just asked the crystal to help the other one to do some extra translating," explained Zalarin.

Costillo re-opened the imagery on the disk, and Aihalaran re-appeared on screen.

"I wish to talk to you now, whoever needs to know this information. My name is Aihalaran, keeper of the records office in the main temple on the northernmost island of

Atlantis.   This information holds the secrets of the energy points and lines over the continent, and of the world. I wish to show you the map of our island first, so you can see where the lines and points of interest lie," said Aihalaran.

With that, he picked up a sheet attached to a board and placed it in front of him.   The island showed steep sided mountains to the south east.   There were more of them a few miles away in the middle of the island, which formed a chain running northwards.   Costillo could see that the land reached far into the north.

"To the northernmost tip, the people who lived there in the earliest times were fair haired with violet eyes," said Aihalaran, "to the south, the people were blue eyed but with red hair.   To the south east, there was a very large portal within the mountain ring, as they called it.   There was a temple there, situated just to the north of a rocky knoll, called the temple dedicated to Elaharia.

She was, and still is the angelic being who lives there, and she actively inspired all to the temple. This portal takes people to different time zones very easily because, with the area being igneous, there are especially huge crystals under that point.

People have gone back to Lemurean times and even further back.   They may have also gone forwards in time too, we don't know. The rule is that in travelling, you always go back in time to the same place you were at before you travelled, and hope that the land you were on when you began your travel has not disappeared, en route, and you would find yourself in the middle of an ocean!"

"You can stop the machine there, Costillo. I think we have enough to go," said Zalarin, "Andal and everyone! You can continue looking for other portals and sites, as it is important in case others are awakening."

Costillo rose from his seat and went over to Zalarin.

"Can I travel back in time to find Maraya?" asked Costillo, "I have our crystal here?"

"Wait!" said Zalarin, "Firstly, I wish to contact Anchorin and tell him what we've discovered, come!"

In Zalarin's small office, not unlike Anchorin's, Zalarin activated his crystal and Anchorin's face appeared, hovering over the top of it.

"It's a serious problem," said Anchorin, "but as we are practiced in time travel, we should manage. Can you show

38

me where exactly this portal is? I can get my trusty friend Hudlath to investigate."

Zalarin picked up a pen, sheet of paper, and something to lean the paper on, and held them near the crystal.

"Here are the Summer Islands area of mountains," and Zalarin sketched the ring of mountains boldly, "here is the rocky knoll in the centre. The site of the old temple is to the north, where the sea temple is now. To the south west of the knoll, that is where the vortex is, and it has crystals beneath it which transport people to the past times at a moment's notice."

"I see," said Anchorin, "I shall tell Hudlath, and he'll probably go very soon. Don't worry Costillo, Maraya simply may not be able to return without her crystal."

"There is one thing that Aihalaran said, that people may have also gone forward in time, but they didn't know if they did," said Zalarin, "it sounds possible that it may only be a one way vortex, that is, only going back in time."

"What would be the good of that," cried Costillo, "everyone would get stuck!"

"Yes indeed, however, there are always other ways to return, and there are other vortices that would do that job, and of course, the crystals we have will be suitable for the job," replied Zalarin, "Anchorin, you will tell Hudlath to contact us once he is on his way, won't you?"

"I shall, Zalarin, in fact it would be better if I ask him to visit you before he travels back in time," said Anchorin.

"That will be ideal, thank you, my friend," replied Zalarin.

"I'll look forward to meeting Hudlath again, despite being concerned about Maraya," said Costillo.

"He's been on many missions, and so he is well practiced," replied Zalarin.

Chapter 3 – Hudlath Time Travels to the North Island

There was a jovial reunion between Anchorin and Hudlath in the mountain temple's meeting room.

"I know it hasn't been that long really, it just feels a long time!" said Hudlath.

"What have you been doing in my office two hundred years ahead during that time?" asked Anchorin wryly.

"Just doing dutiful jobs, sending energy for the vortices to open and for spring to return as you'd expect, in _my_ office!" responded Hudlath, and they laughed together. Then simultaneously, their faces became serious.

"We must do our part to rescue Maraya," said Hudlath, "is it getting warmer in the valleys?"

"Indeed it is, a warm spring day, though I expect it's a bit cool still with you," asked Anchorin.

"Yes, plants are just beginning to stir ever so slightly, and the snows are receding, but don't let's just talk about the weather!" replied Hudlath.

"To business!" exclaimed Anchorin, "I have talked to Zanadar, and he is on the lookout too."

They walked out of the meeting room, and wandered towards the entrance, still discussing details.

"Good luck my friend," said Anchorin, "you won't use the vortex itself will you?"

"Not at all, I shall analyse it with my crystal and travel parallel to its path to see where it goes, and should be able to detect the whole route," said Hudlath, "and I hope to anticipate a clue of Maraya's whereabouts, but I don't feel it will be straightforward, do you?

Anchorin shook his head, "I'm afraid not."

"I'll contact you or get messages through to you as and when I can, of course, my friend," said Hudlath.

Anchorin gave affirmation and patted Hudlath's shoulder. Hudlath departed from the summit, and went swiftly down the slopes on a mountain buggy as fast as it would go. Once in Chalidocea, Hudlath obtained a hoverbuggy, and asked to go to the sea temple. En route he saw the first spring flush of fresh foliage and emerging flowers.

'Ah! There goes a pegasus', he thought, watching its graceful movements as it arced through the sky over towards where Jadeir and the nature spirits all lived.

Once at the stopping point by the beach, he made haste across the sands, half gliding and half walking.

'There's still not quite enough earth energy to fly properly as yet,' he thought.

"Is Zalarin there, please? I'm Hudlath," he announced to the first priest he saw.

"I'll call for him now," replied the priest, "but please come in and make yourself comfortable here in the entrance while you wait."

The priest directed Hudlath to a few seats just inside the entrance, in a little alcove.

Zalarin and Costillo soon came through, and they shook hands with Hudlath, and sat down on the remaining available seats.

"My friends, I shall use my crystal, following the line of direction the vortex takes, and by checking each of the time periods every so often. I shall contact you as frequently as I can; and I said I'd do the same for Anchorin, but if need be, I shall only send messages to one either of you or via Zanadar," said Hudlath, "you do know Zanadar, don't you?"

"Yes, I know of him, but never spoken to him or met him as yet," replied Zalarin, "how do you contact him?"

"Just think of Anchorin, then their spaceship and then Zanadar. It usually gets you through. If not, just get Anchorin to call him, and then he will contact you easily enough," explained Hudlath.

"You did get all the details of what happened when Maraya disappeared didn't you?" asked Costillo, "there's nothing else you need to know?"

"No, it's fine, Costillo, I have enough information for now," replied Hudlath, and then he announced, "and I'm ready to depart!"

He gave Costillo a reassuring pat on the shoulder, and then Zalarin took Hudlath down to the sailing vessel.

"Here, Hudlath, take this crystal to operate the vessel, it may be prudent to have an extra crystal, for your investigations!" remarked Zalarin.

"Thank you my friend," smiled Hudlath.

He put the crystal in the slot by the vessel's engine, jumped into it with agility and sailed off, giving Zalarin a parting wave. Zalarin watched him go, as if trying to intuit the outcome.

Hudlath noticed the two temple dolphins following the vessel.

"Hello my friends," said Hudlath to the dolphins who were now swimming alongside him, and they came to the surface and began chattering.

"You'll show me where it happened will you? From a safe distance, thank you!" he replied.

As they approached the island of Elaharia, the dolphins headed around to the south-westerly side, and soon began chattering again as they approached the area.

"I see, my friends, just about four dolphin lengths away!" said Hudlath, "I shall go and land the vessel on a nearby part of the island, and then start travelling back in time, thank you my friends."

Hudlath glided over to the shore and moored the vessel, which would be rendered invisible when he became invisible too, and he removed the crystal in case it was needed. He found a satisfactory level place after some clambering, as the south-western side of Elaharia was a bit steeper than where Maraya and Costillo had been on the eastern side. The dolphins raised themselves out of the water and called to him as Hudlath prepared himself. He took out some of the blue mist plant, usually used by time travellers to become temporarily invisible to safeguard themselves against any unexpected situations.

Hudlath waved to the dolphins, took some of the blue mist tincture and disappeared. With his crystal in hand, he focused a moment, working out which time period to visit.

'Hm, I'll just return to my time and see what happens with the vortex,' he thought.

He focused on the date and time of day, projecting that thought onto the crystal. It glowed strongly, and to him his surroundings began to shimmer and blur, whereas for anyone else, if he were visible, he would be a shimmering blur to them. Then, when he reached his time period two hundred years ahead; the crystal stopped the projection through time. Hudlath looked at the vortex and the surroundings.

'The shimmering energy around the vortex area is not visible here; it can't be active in the future. Right, I'll have to go back in time then,' he thought.

Once more he set his crystal.

"I'll return back in time, setting the crystal to go back every one hundred years and examine the vortex as I go,' he thought.

Everything blurred again. The vortex's energy grew increasingly stronger. He looked around once everything became clear.

'I can see that this vortex is growing wider, the further back in time I go, it's going to be a problem, for I shall have to avoid being enveloped by it, and if the vessel is too, if I'm not in it, it may disappear and get lost in an unstable vortex. I'll ask the dolphins to steer the boat away back to the sea temple for now."

He thought intently of Zalarin and shortly made contact with him.

"Zalarin, I am only one hundred years back in the past. The vortex is definitely linked to the past, but the problem is that the capacity of it is widening as I proceed. I shall have to send the vessel back to your sea temple; perhaps the dolphins could take it? I can't get through to them, but maybe you can?" asked Hudlath.

"I shall try Hudlath, I can see them outside the temple now. I'll tell them, I presume you've kept the crystal. We have plenty more replacements, but if the vortex expands to encompass the island wouldn't it really be better to travel back in the vessel?" suggested Zalarin.

"Yes, maybe you're right. I'd better do that. I'm not usually keen on travelling with water around me, it's not very stable!" replied Hudlath, "but I have no option."

"I'll send the dolphins back anyway, as they could be there for you in case of difficulties, if you have to return quickly," commented Zalarin.

"Yes, all right, I'll just return to get into the vessel first, and then revert back in time. Goodbye for now, my friend" replied Hudlath.

There was a blur forward in time, and Hudlath clambered back down the hill and set off in the vessel, 'a good twenty dolphin lengths away', he thought, hoping that would suffice. He travelled backward two hundred years, and by that he could measure the vortex's expansion.

'It was two Atlantean human widths across originally, and in one hundred years it expanded to six human widths. Now it has expanded to twelve human widths, so, on average it is six human widths for every hundred years. I'll just keep on going further back, while ensuring I'm well away from that vortex!'

Hudlath set it for six hundred years back in time, and saw that it was beginning to encroach on the island. He set the crystal

43

for another six hundred years back, and the vortex was encroaching on part of the hill, but still, there was little change.

'Perhaps I shall have to link back to when this continent was above water. Hm, the date was 8,400 years ago according to the records, taking the date to 20,400BC by the twenty first century dating system. I'll just move further away as the coastline protruded further out,' thought Hudlath.

He meditated a moment and decided to sail further south by a couple of miles, though they were Atlantean miles, since the Atlanteans were twice the size of people in recent times, and also the dolphins were larger in size, for that matter.

Hudlath recalled a time when he had once travelled in time to view the Ice Age, and reckoned that many of the Atlantean giant descendants had perished then, due to the extreme cold, and inability to adapt. Many remains were not evident as there were creatures around then that chewed bones as well as everything else. Hudlath almost shuddered at that thought, as well as with the biting cold when he had gone there. He had found himself on a small island surrounded by a stormy and icy sea a veritable arctic ocean. Mildly horrified, he swiftly set his sights on earlier times within seconds!

Once in a satisfactory position, he set his crystal 8,400 years back in time, and prayed that he would miss the cataclysmic effect of land and water movements. He prepared himself in case of a quick need to move again swiftly once he arrived.

There! The blurring was slowing down, the vessel was lifted out of the water, and he found himself on a long beach. The vortex by now was immense, and covered the whole of the northern Atlantean island where the mountain ring was, and just beyond. Hudlath exhaled and his intense expression of concentration relaxed.

'What a relief I arrived safely! I'll just hide the vessel between these rocks and then report to Zalarin.'

"Zalarin, it's Hudlath. I've travelled back to when the northern island was above the sea! I've just secured the vessel and am off to investigate now. The vortex is now over the whole mountain ring area. I don't know as yet of course, whether Maraya will be here, or further back in time. I'll be in contact with you when I know more, goodbye Zalarin," he said.

"If the vortex is covering the whole island then you'll have to enter it, Hudlath!" questioned Zalarin.

"Yes, I know Zalarin, but I can see people in the distance all doing their daily activities there, so it must be alright at this time period, my friend," replied Hudlath.

"Alright Hudlath. Goodbye, thank you, and good luck," said Zalarin.

Hudlath moved off, still invisible, and managed to hover along a little, periodically, to speed up his progress. Once across the sands, he arrived at the knoll, where there were priests of all calibres all around. The land between Elaharia and the mountain ring, which would be submerged later on, was very fertile, and was being farmed diligently by many lay priests.

Hudlath looked everywhere for traces of Maraya's whereabouts, but to no avail at present. He realised that he had just entered the vortex, but hadn't felt any effect. Once round the knoll he saw the original temple where the sea temple site would be. Hudlath walked over to it as quietly as he could, and tried his best to keep his thoughts entirely silent or else he might have been detected. He ascended the entrance stairs and began searching. He knew that the language was completely different to later Atlantean, and the clothes they wore were more natural colours like the assistant Ailaharan, though Hudlath hadn't seen the information on the disk.

He decided to blend in by finding the clothes laundry room, where priests were diligently cleaning them for the whole temple. He wandered invisibly past some working priests who were talking together while rinsing some garments. Hudlath spotted a cupboard nearby and opened the door gently, while watching the priests to ensure his movements weren't noticed, and he took a top and trousers. He wandered off and found a room to change; he folded his clothes and cloak, and put them in his bag, which he then slung over his shoulder. He only retained his staff, but had removed his headband, since a high priest would attract far too much attention.

'Time to appear!' he thought ruefully, and hope I can make myself understood.'

He came out of the room and crept back to the main corridor, which was milling with busy priests. Some were returning from their agricultural work, others were going out to do their shift, and a few were busily moving here and there carrying crystals or papers around with them. Hudlath was happy that

45

he had not been noticed too much initially, as he strode off equally purposefully with the intention of talking to one of the higher members of the priesthood.

It was more luck than anything else that he noticed the sign on a door a little way along the main corridor, which was depicted in a similar pictorial language to Egyptian writing, of a figure with a head dress on like a pharaoh, holding an ankh and flails crossed over each other. The door was, like all the doors in the temple, shaped like eastern doors with an arched apex.

He knocked on the door, and when he heard the response, Hudlath entered, hoping that the high priest wouldn't be too suspicious of a complete stranger entering his temple. The high priest behind his office table looked up, eyeing the newcomer curiously.

"What brings you here, and first of all, who are you?" asked the high priest, looking sternly.

Hudlath found it difficult to understand the language, but by linking into the Garden of Eden swiftly, they helped him to overcome the language barrier, and it was as if he knew it all instantly, and somehow was able to reply in their language quite easily.

"I am a high priest myself, from lands far away on another continent, and I have the proof in my bag. My name is Hudlath, and I am skilled in scrying and healing, as well as the usual requirements of a high priest," he explained.

"I wish to see the proof before I can trust you," replied the high priest.

Hudlath brought out his garments and the headband, and placed them on the high priest's table.

"You may have stolen these as well as the cloak you are wearing, but as we don't know of anywhere that has such clothes, I think you must be telling the truth. Put your hand on this truth crystal. If it turns gold you are truthful, but if it turns dark, then I shall know," he said, and he summoned his attendant priests, who entered from an adjoining room, "keep guard by the door as we have a stranger."

Hudlath put his hand on the crystal and it turned gold.

"Ah! So you are truthful, my friend," said the high priest and he visibly relaxed, and so did the guarding priests, and he dismissed them with a smile, "my name is Melcharin, so what brings you here to our parts?" he asked.

"I am looking for a friend called Maraya," explained Hudlath, as he quietly replaced his clothing into his bag again, "she has long dark hair, brown eyes, and is quite young; she is also a high ranking priestess."

Hudlath paused to think of further information he could offer, especially such as why she had wandered off so far.

"Why did she travel so far from her homeland, when she would have her duties in her temple?" Melcharin asked, looking slightly puzzled.

"Apparently, she was looking for herbs, for we are lacking in one or two species that are difficult to maintain growth over a period of time, so we sometimes send people to either look for them, or seek out other possible plants to add to our collection," answered Hudlath.

Melcharin paused for thought.

"Why send out a high ranking priestess, and what are these herbs that are so rare?" he asked.

Hudlath had to think fast, "Maraya went because she is one of the most knowledgeable of the priesthood on such matters, and she has done journeys of this sort before, she also communicates her knowledge to other temples in order to share it. As for the plants; the gift of oratory plant, mortal healing plant and the gifts of spirit plant," replied Hudlath, "I presume they are growing around here?"

"Why yes, they are common here, as I understand them to be everywhere I know of," replied Melcharin, looking slightly surprised, "I can't imagine such plants being rare at all. Maraya sounds to be quite an unusual asset and worth looking for."

"I'm afraid the plants are scarce with us, for many peoples from afar visited our lands, which are in the north east of Atlantis; who were in need of much healing since we have always been renowned for it. Unfortunately we ran very low in supplies. We thought that seed stocks in other areas of the island would be found, but to no avail, for they had run out too with our demands," replied Hudlath.

Melcharin nodded, "well my friend, you are welcome to take some plants with you, but we have seen no sign of your priestess Maraya so far, can you show an image of what she looks like?"

Hudlath pointed his crystal at the nearest wall of the office, looked up an image of Maraya within it and projected it onto the wall.

"No, I'm sorry I don't know of her at all," responded Melcharin, "but I can contact other temples across the island and see if anyone replies with an affirmative response, if I could have that image transferred onto my crystal?"

Hudlath immediately projected the image onto Melcharin's crystal he had placed onto the table.

"Just go outside and obtain what you wish in the way of plants. Better still, I'll call Gadar, he's the head of the plant tending priests." Melcharin reached for his crystal and focused on Gadar, and his face was visible around the crystal. "Gadar, would you escort our friend Hudlath to the herb garden, so he can take a few plants, as in his lands they are scarce, please can you come now?"

"Yes Melcharin, I can," replied Gadar.

Hudlath rose from his seat, shook Melcharin's hand and bowed, "I shall return your clothes soon, for I will have to move elsewhere if Maraya isn't here."

"Yes indeed, although you are welcome to stay the night and eat with us, before you might wish to do so," said Melcharin graciously.

Hudlath thanked him and departed with Gadar when he came. Meanwhile, Melcharin contacted temples nationally.

Later, Hudlath returned to the temple with the plants, and left them beside the entrance in a woven bag. He walked along to Melcharin's office and knocked on the door, and entered when he heard the answer.

"Ah! My friend Hudlath!" he exclaimed, "there have been no sightings of Maraya yet, but I still have a few temples to hear from. I think you ought to at least stay for one night; you are welcome here. I shall personally show you to your quarters."

He led Hudlath past a few more doors around a corner and up some steps. Melcharin entered through the door to a beautiful and spacious room.

"My quarters are not far away, and there are washing facilities in here too. Some food will be brought to your room. The meal that we all eat communally is during the day. I'll see you to speak to in the morning, but we do have a sunset ceremony, giving thanks to the great creator for everything provided during this day," said Melcharin.

"I'd like to come," replied Hudlath, and then Melcharin left.

Hudlath explored the room closely, and then contacted Zalarin, speaking very quietly.

"Zalarin! This is Hudlath, I am here in the temple, still in the time period of 8,400 years ago, and have been invited to stay the night by Melcharin the high priest. There's no sign of Maraya and several temples have reported they don't know of her whereabouts so far."

"Maybe she went elsewhere. Is Melcharin trustworthy enough? Perhaps Anchorin would know of him more than me as to his character. If he doesn't prove worthy, I wouldn't stay there!" replied Zalarin.

Hudlath indicated that he'd contact Anchorin. Soon, Anchorin's face was visible around Hudlath's crystal.

"Anchorin, I'm on north island back 8,400 years or 20,400BC, in the old temple on Elaharia, and the vortex covers to the mountain circle, but there's no danger. The high priest is Melcharin, and I've been invited to stay the night. He's contacted all the temples and some have reported back and not known of Maraya as yet. Do you know anything about him? Maraya may well be in another time zone however," asked Hudlath in a low voice.

"I'll find out, it won't take long, Hudlath," said Anchorin, and his image faded instantly.

Hudlath hurriedly put the crystal away, for he heard someone approach the door, so he sat down on the seat by the window and tried to look as though he'd been there for a while, just resting.

There was an announcement of food, and Hudlath asked the priest to enter, which he did; and the food was carefully placed on the central round table. The priest smiled kindly and then departed. Hudlath used his crystal to dowse the food to ensure it would be safe to eat.

'Though I feel relatively safe here, there is a slight nagging doubt, though,' he thought.

Though he refrained from thinking it out verbally, and more like a conscious acknowledgement of this, for he didn't want to draw attention to his thoughts of suspicion by any priests, in case any of them were actively keeping an eye on him.

He looked out of the window and noticed the sun was low in the sky, and that priests were now filing outside, to arrange themselves into concentric circles. Hudlath got up, and ensured his belongings were safely hidden in the room before going outside to join them.

Once he had mingled with the others within the circles they all stood quietly for a moment, stilling themselves internally.

Then they all turned to face the setting sun, while retaining their circular formation. They raised their arms high and began to chant in a low, gentle voice, and a single phrase was repeated several times. Hudlath understood it to be a blessing to the sun. Then they lowered their arms and faced the centre where Melcharin stood, directing the ceremony.

"Think of our world surrounded by peace, and that the power of the spiritual realms will oust all that isn't required in our world. May the tower of energy surround us all, and bless us and our lands," preached Melcharin.

Hudlath wondered about the tower of energy and what the 'all that isn't required' referred to, and whether Anchorin or Zalarin would know from their archive material. He decided to contact them later.

The sun began to sink below the horizon, and the orange tinged sky mellowed to pale yellow. Then the ceremony was concluded, and everyone silently filed back indoors. There were cups filled with fruit juice awaiting the priests on a table in the main corridor, and they took one each and departed to their rooms. Hudlath did likewise, swiftly went upstairs to his room and closed the door.

He waited until the sound of footsteps had abated before he made contact with his colleagues.

"Anchorin!" he whispered, "I wish to ask you to make an investigation."

Hudlath wrote down what he wished to investigate or know about in a notebook that he always carried with him wherever he went, and would be entering the 'tower of energy' topic shortly.

"I'll get back to you as soon as I can!" said Anchorin, also whispering, "return if you need to escape, my friend."

Anchorin's face had a pertinent look to it, and Hudlath wondered why he would need to return since everything was so quiet and peaceful at the ancient temple. He sipped at the juice, pondering on the day's events and watched the sun's rays fade completely.

'Maybe I'll use the crystal to focus on other parts of Atlantis,' he thought, without verbalising it.

He drew out his crystal again and focused outside the circle of the mountains. The crystal picked up a view of a strange dark haze with pinpoints of light here and there. He still wondered where Maraya went, and what clues could indicate a previous time period where she could be found.

'Should I chance going back in time from here?' he thought, 'no, I'll just leave it until tomorrow and hope Melcharin has some news.'

Hudlath's crystal glowed, so he picked it up, and Anchorin's face appeared.

"Hudlath, that tower of energy is to keep out dark forces at work, which will topple the northern island of Atlantis soon enough," he explained.

"No wonder I feel a sense of unrest here," Hudlath replied.

Hudlath also explained that he'd scryed beyond the mountain ring and saw the dark haze too, and that Maraya still concerned him.

"I think Melcharin is on our side, Hudlath, but their culture doesn't know anything about time travel any more, and just enough about energy use to hold out against the dark forces on Atlantis, but for how long? They may well have to emigrate. As for Maraya, if she's been moving outside the temple; she actually may have thought to walk along to where the land of the north island is at its nearest to our island, and hope to find a way to cross over, or find another vortex en route. See if you can find any more information Hudlath, though if not apparent, you will have to travel further back in time," said Anchorin.

"Yes Anchorin, I will await Melcharin's news tomorrow, and if nothing more, I'll move on and go further back in time," replied Hudlath.

They concluded their discussion and Hudlath settled down to go to sleep, sending his prayers in hope for clues of Maraya's whereabouts.

In his dreams he saw himself holding his crystal. He saw a vivid image in it of Maraya looking at him, suffused with a beautiful smile, yet behind her a strange landscape he had never envisaged before. There were incandescent lights, beings moving around who were half visible, and he seemed overwhelmed by the force of energy that emanated from the crystal that he fell over backwards unconscious. When he came to, the crystal was still in his hand, but all the images had faded, and only a pulsating silvery glow remained around him.

Hudlath awoke, and to his surprise, he found that it was morning.

'I feel as if I'd only just gone to bed! Oh! And that dream!' he thought, which brought it all back to his mind, 'perhaps she's gone to another planet. I'll tell Anchorin about it.'

He dressed himself and gathered his few belongings together. There was the customary knock, and food was provided again, which he happily ate. Afterwards Hudlath went to find Melcharin in his office, and he knocked on his door.

"Good morning my friend," said Melcharin, "the answer is that I have not found any evidence of your friend here. So what will you do?" and he looked searchingly at Hudlath, who looked pensive.

"I shall move westwards I think," Hudlath said thoughtfully, "I have an old friend who lives in that direction, a high priest called Anchorin."

"I've not heard that name before. Some of my people have travelled west, and they met one or two high priests called Talaran and Beuran, and they were very helpful when we had need of counsel or supplies. Have you met them?" asked Melcharin.

"They sound most useful for travellers to know, but I haven't met them or heard of them until now. Perhaps Anchorin does, and I shall ask him. Thank you very much for your hospitality and I shall recommend you to anyone of good intent that I meet. I presume most people are trustworthy?" asked Hudlath, hoping to know more about the characteristic state of the present times there.

Melcharin paused a moment, "just ask them to consider whether they prefer all that is good in life and whether the creator stirs their every move."

"What if they say it doesn't?" answered Hudlath.

"The very occasional person who does respond like that is likely to be a lazy person, which I'm sure can be found in any society," replied Melcharin, "and best avoided as you'd expect."

"Yes, I shall follow your advice my friend, thank you," said Hudlath graciously.

He shook hands with Melcharin and went to the door to leave.

"Don't forget your plants!" prompted Melcharin.

"Thank you, I won't," replied Hudlath with a smile.

He walked to the entrance and picked up the plants. He then wandered down towards a pathway nearby, which took him in an easterly direction, and he strode off swiftly. He intended to find a place further on where he could become invisible again, and then return to the vessel and make contact with Anchorin before travelling again.

"Anchorin!" said an invisible Hudlath, "I have left Melcharin's temple, as there have been no sitings of Maraya, but I had a vivid dream last night of seeing Maraya's face in my crystal."
He told Anchorin all the details and wondered whether to return to Chalidocea or go back further in time to see the vortex's origins, and that she had gone via that moment in time.
"It may take me back to the source of where Maraya departed from," said Hudlath.
"Are you sure about this Hudlath, for if you go too, we won't know how to get you both back," said Anchorin.
"Don't worry, I'll ensure that I stay outside the vortex, so I can observe without getting drawn in," replied Hudlath, "perhaps
Zanadar and his friends could then follow up the lead provided by the vortex, and see where it takes them to?"
"That sounds a logical idea, I shall ask them to do that," responded Anchorin. There was a long pause. "Are you feeling all right Hudlath?
Hudlath had become a bit dizzy and his voice reflected that.
"I don't know what happened. I'm usually perfectly healthy and alert when I time travel, it must be something to do with that vortex, which I may find out about once I reach its source," replied Hudlath.
"How are the people there, health-wise?" asked Anchorin.
"They are perfectly healthy, though on reflection, now that I am away from the vortex, they did appear to be dreamy, and don't appear to be worried about what lies beyond the tower of energy. They have no apparent strategies in place in case of any hostile forces attacking them, unless those in charge do have contingency plans that they are keeping to themselves, and don't reveal them to the lower ranks or strangers. Though my intuition told me it was the former," explained Hudlath, "Also, Melcharin seemed to imply that most people were god orientated outside his temple, and that anyone who wasn't was only lazy. I found it hard to believe that concept, unless he had something to hide. I shall go back in time anyway, as I am not far from the vessel, so I shall contact you when I make further discoveries, Anchorin."

"I see; what apparent innocence in the face of impending danger!" and Anchorin looked concerned and gave a wry expression, "go carefully my friend," he replied.

"I shall! Farewell," responded Hudlath.

Hudlath went to sit in the vessel so that it would become invisible too, having enveloped it within 'the shield', as Atlanteans called it. To quote Hudlath when talking to his student priests; 'to explain that concept of the shield more fully, it is when an idea, object or concept is encompassed or overlit by an umbrella concept, manoeuvre, idea, energy or organisation.'

He began to consider how much further in time he wished to go, as he motored away from the land completely. He reached for his crystal and looked at it intently, formulating the thought 'where in time is Maraya?' He visualised a blue light around the crystal and a golden glow around that. He half-closed his eyes and scryed; strangely, he saw a fleeting image of Maraya's hair turning fair, with Alyssia's face alongside. 'Curious!' he thought.

Chapter 4 – The Discovery

Alyssia had just finished another painting recently; it depicted a crystalline cave by the sea, and Kenny, who owned the New Age Shop Plas Myrddin had enthusiastically put it on the wall.

She had spent the day pondering on the next image to inspire her.

"Karin, I'm just going to take my sketchbook and go to the hill fort, I need some inspiration," said Alyssia.

"That's ok! I'm up to my eyes in paperwork!" said Karin, Kenny's partner, who turned around and gave Alyssia a sunny smile; "we'll see you later."

"Bye then!" said Alyssia, "oh, would you want anything from the shops when I return, since Sarah will be returning much later?"

"We've got plenty, but perhaps some more Old Oswestry tartlets, since a certain person keeps walking off with more than his fair share!" replied Karin.

"I'll get a large supply," laughed Alyssia.

She departed through the flat door and down the stairwell to the outside door, where her car was parked. She set off along the little B road in a northerly direction, and parked at the lay by on the west side of the hill fort, and then she walked up the slight incline to its flat expanse. The weather was quite mild for a December day, and Alyssia found herself standing in a place near the centre of the hill fort, and she turned to face the sun.

A sudden flash of white light came, which surprised Alyssia and made her think of the time in Atlantis that she, Karin, Kenny and Sarah had all gone back to originally on the first trip. Suddenly the face of Maraya appeared, and seemed to be beckoning Alyssia towards her, and so she instinctively approached, and found she had walked into the portal at the centre of the hill fort. Alyssia, Karin and Sarah were aware of portals and energy centres, as a number of others were, who were spiritually orientated, but on this occasion, the light quickly became very powerful after the flash of light, and Maraya's appearance. Alyssia had to step back out of the vortex very quickly, as she thought she was going to be projected somewhere else.

'I'm not even prepared to go to Atlantis, not without my crystal and necessary potions!' she thought.

Despite that, she saw an image of a dolphin appearing in the vortex, and she sat close by to the vortex despite her misgivings and looked up at it. The dolphin looked at her intently, and its eyes shone like crystals, reflecting sunlight, and a stream of strangely unintelligible phenomena, as Alyssia initially called it, came rushing towards her mind, charged with a collection of unearthly symbols, glyphs and unusual sensations, the like of which she found it impossible to describe.

Once this surge completed itself, the dolphin faded, leaving only a feeling of love in Alyssia's heart. She sat for a while thinking about it, feeling dazed. She was still seeing after-images of those glyphs and symbols, and her head seemed to throb, and felt disorientated.

'I feel as if I have information inside me that is somehow reconstituting itself and me, so that it can become intelligible,' she thought.

Despite the mild December weather, she was feeling extra cold standing there, and so she quietly returned back to the lay by beside the hill fort, and drove back to the flat. As she went, flashes of the white light appeared in front of her eyes, and the fleeting image of a dolphin's tail appeared, swooping upwards as if the pale wintry sky had turned into a turquoise sea, and then it disappeared into the far distance, as if heading home to the stars. Alyssia had briefly parked while the dolphin image had appeared. Once back at the flat, Alyssia got out of her car and was greeted by the smell of food from a restaurant.

'Oh, the tartlets! Glad I remembered!' she thought, though their familiarity seemed strangely incongruous after her unearthly experiences, but the sudden humour of it somehow reassured her.

"Thanks Alyssia!" said Karin, "did you have an inspiring time at the fort?" and she looked up cheerfully, but began to notice a slight disorientation in Alyssia's eyes, and her face grew more serious.

"Yes I did," answered Alyssia hesitantly, "it was amazing, but at the same time, it is proving to be strange. You see, it was as if I was given a strange, unearthly energy and language which is now inside me, but I don't know what it is yet, and is making me feel pretty disorientated."

Alyssia gave a full explanation of all the details of the event, and said she'd tell Kenny later.

"That was also strange that you saw Maraya's face too, and the dolphins are linked to the Pleiades, of course, so it must be Pleiadean language that you experienced?" asked Karin, thoughtfully, "you must just take time out to rest if you need to, to sort this out, Alyssia."

Alyssia gave Karin a hug, "I'll just record everything that happened, it's always helpful and gets things a little straighter in your mind," she said, and then went to her room.

Sarah had arrived in Cornwall several days ago, for her tenants had moved out of her cottage near Zennor, due to the forthcoming house sale. Geraldine, her healer friend had brought Sarah's things over that she'd stored at her house in St Just. They gathered the last of Sarah's belongings and took them to the car.

"Goodbye Geraldine, dear," said Sarah, hugging her friend, "thank you for all your help."

"I'll try to get up and see you sometime, Sarah, perhaps in the summer," replied Geraldine.

"You'd better!" said Sarah, with a hand on Geraldine's shoulder.

"An offer I can't refuse, then!" responded Geraldine, "But you'll miss your herbs, Sarah!"

"Yes, initially, but I have a large stock of seeds and a few cuttings in the boot for the next place! I've decided on finding somewhere to the west of Oswestry," replied Sarah.

"Sounds good dear, off you go!" said Geraldine cheerfully.

Sarah got in her car and switched on the engine.

"Just help yourself to any herbs before you go! Goodbye dear!" said Sarah, blowing a kiss, before driving away, and they waved to each other.

Geraldine looked at the sold sign and thought how remarkably quickly she had sold the property.

'Well, back to St Just for those two clients coming for their massages this afternoon!' she thought, as she helped herself to some handfuls of herbs.

Dusk was approaching and Sarah pulled off from the main road and found a lay-by. For precautionary measures, she locked the car doors and then produced her mobile phone and dialled.

"Hello Karin, it's Sarah! I'm just south of the Shrewsbury bypass by about five miles," she said.

"Oh good! We'll expect to see you in about half an hour, with any luck," said Karin.

"With any luck!" echoed Sarah with a chuckle.

"Will start on a meal shortly, just a bit more paperwork to finish off. See you later," said Karin.

"Looking forward!" said Sarah, "bye!"

She put the phone away and did a U turn, and then sped off back to the A458.

"I'd definitely recommend this one! Though they're all excellent, as I wouldn't stock anything inferior. It happens to be my personal favourite," said Kenny, whose shock of curly hair and animated face was always appealing to young people.

"Why haven't you got yours on today?" asked one boy.

"Ah well, I left it upstairs, but I'll wear it tomorrow, I promise!" he said emphatically.

'I wish they'd buy these ethnic friendship bracelets instead of looking at them and trying them on,' he thought.

"Right! I think we should all start a friendship club, boys and girls!" he said dramatically, "I'll be big friendship chief, and you'll all be my cubs, how about that! And now is the time for you to join!" he said. He gave them all a penetrating stare, but with his shock of hair and big moustache, it only made them laugh.

"Go on then!" said one boy at last, "I'll get one, big friendly chief!"

"And so will I!" said another.

"That's the spirit!" chortled Kenny.

Before long, they were all clamouring for them.

There was the sound of a doorbell, and Karin ran downstairs to the back door.

"Sarah, dear!" exclaimed Karin, and gave her a hug, "come in!"

"Thank you," said Sarah, wearily, "I don't think I'd like to do that journey again in a hurry!"

By the time Sarah was upstairs and putting her hand luggage in her room, Kenny had shut the shop and come upstairs.

"Where's the tea then?" he said, smiling, "has Sarah arrived, I thought I heard some sounds on the stairs?"

"Yes, she'll be coming through shortly," replied Karin.

"Did she get her luggage in?" he asked.

"No, not yet, dear," replied Karin.

"Well, I'll get it then, no one will feel like it later," he said.

He walked down the corridor to the bedrooms, and knocked on Sarah's door, then heard the sound of voices from Alyssia's room.

"Hello girls, your personal assistant will collect your luggage for you ma'am!" he cried.

The door flew open, and Sarah's head peeked out, with Alyssia close behind.

"Hello boyo!" they said in unison.

"Hello fair maidens!" said Kenny in a Welsh accent. He gave Sarah a hug, "glad you're here safely, let me have your keys!"

Sarah went to get them from her bag and handed them over with a smile, and he went off to her car. By the time he had returned with a huge load, Karin and Alyssia were dishing up the tea.

"I wish Jadeir was here, he'd probably get all the cases to fly upstairs!" remarked Kenny.

"And save you the value of some exercise!" answered Karin.

"Thanks, dear!" said Kenny obliquely out of the corner of his mouth, "can you point me in a northerly direction?"

Karin put her hands around Kenny's waist and tweaked him until he was facing down the corridor to the bedrooms.

"Luggage ahoy!" shouted Kenny.

Sarah came out of her room and directed Kenny inside, having taken the boxes from in front of his face!

"How did you manage to get all that upstairs, Kenny?" asked Sarah.

"It was in the early days when we were just starting up, and needed to get a lot of stock of course, but I ordered so much one time, that we didn't have enough room for it downstairs, so I had to bring it into the flat. In fact, we had a power cut on the day it was delivered, so we got to know where all the corners and places to bump into were!" explained Kenny.

"Is that everything?" asked Sarah, as she examined her boxes, "no, there's a few more things aren't there?"

"Don't worry, I'll get them," insisted Kenny, "dinner is being served madam, so just adjourn to the dining room, while I attend to your needs!"

Sarah laughed, following Kenny through to the dining area. Kenny soon returned with the remainder of the belongings, and then joined the others at the table.

"Ah, it's nice to get back to telepathy again, you know, talking is so much more of an effort!" said Kenny.

"Yes, it certainly is," replied Sarah, emphatically.

They all began eating their meal, and there were murmurs of appreciation all round, especially from Sarah and Kenny.

"I wonder why you saw Maraya's image in that vortex?" asked Kenny thoughtfully.

"And why with dolphins, and also why you saw it?" asked Sarah.

"Maybe because I was a priestess in a sea temple, as she was, the one quite near Anchorin's mountain, and I am also associated with dolphins since they came to the temple ceremonies," replied Alyssia.

"But all those symbols," remarked Karin.

"Yes, I know, perhaps Maraya instigated it; the linking up of the dolphins with me in order to experience all of this," said Alyssia.

"Are you still getting the flashing lights and phenomena at present?" asked Kenny.

"It's not so intense," and she told Kenny about it all. "It's eased off at present, but I hope I get to know what it's all about," said Alyssia, "soon enough!"

"It sounds as though it could become a bit intensive Alyssia, dear, don't wish for it to happen in too much of a hurry!" remarked Sarah, giving her a pat on the shoulder.

"Yes, you're right really," replied Alyssia, "I'm just so interested to know!"

"I wonder if it means that the connection between ours and other time periods may be opening up?" suggested Kenny.

Everyone looked thoughtful and agreed that it could be possible.

Next morning they were all gathered around the table eating breakfast.

"So, you are looking for a new dwelling place, over to the west, Sarah?" commented Kenny, "I'll be interested to see what you find."

"Can I come over with you to visit some properties, Sarah?" asked Alyssia, "as I'm inbetween paintings at present."

"You're more than welcome, dear," responded Sarah, "all the better for spotting any defects. In fact, I'd like you all to come in due course, to ensure I've got a reliable property, and not an old white elephant!" and she chuckled.

"Don't worry! We'll chase the old elephants off the scene!" replied Kenny, "uh-oh, time to go! It's opening time!"

He got up swiftly, and headed for the flat door with his cup of tea.

"Oh well, you two check out the estate agents, while I do the usual office work here!" said Karin, sighing slightly.

"Ah! We'll bring you a souvenir," said Sarah, and Karin laughed.

Alyssia meanwhile, had gone to her bedroom to fetch something, and returned with her sketchbook.

"I may get some inspiration while I'm out," she said.

"I hope so," replied Karin, sitting down at her desk.

Alyssia gave her a quick hug, as did Sarah, and they left the flat to explore the estate agents' windows.

"Those look interesting, but a bit big, let's enquire inside," said Sarah, and they went indoors.

"Excuse me, I liked two of the properties to the west of Oswestry, but do you have something quite small with a reasonable area of land for growing vegs?" asked Sarah.

The assistant looked at Sarah a moment.

"Funny you should ask, as something has just come in, and not had time to put it up!" she admitted.

She brought out the sheet from her pending file just under the desk on a shelf. Sarah and Alyssia both looked at it. The picture showed a little cottage, a bit run down, but with a patch of land at the front, and a fair sized area at the back with vegetables and fruit trees.

"I like it, where is it?" asked Sarah.

"It's about five miles west of here, between Llansilin and Pen-y-bont, come and look at our map on the wall," said the assistant, going over and pointing to the area.

"Could we view it today?" asked Sarah, having pinpointed the location.

"You're in luck! The estate agent's property viewing manager is available at about 11am," she explained.

"That will be fine. Are there any other little cottages anywhere in this area?" asked Sarah.

"I'm sure there isn't anything else, but I'll ask the property manager when he comes in nearer the time," she replied.

Sarah and Alyssia sped along in Sarah's car to keep sight of the property manager's electric blue Ferrari. The route they took cut across an intricate network of minor roads, taking them through Trefonen. There was a slightly quicker way, but due to road works, they had to go around the south side of a local hill called Mynydd Myfyr, instead of to the north. The route then meandered along, up a sharp incline then down to a T-junction by a river. The Ferrari had already taken a swift right turn, and then a left turn at a crossroads, taking him over the river before parking by the cottage.

Once they had parked there too, they got out and approached the front door.

"Not bad, Alyssia!" said Sarah, eagerly.

"Although it's by the road, it's quite secluded behind that hedge and with those two cherry trees," said the property manager, opening the door, "welcome to Ty Bach Craig, which means the small house by the rock!" and he pointed over to a crag opposite the cottage.

He showed them all the rooms, and there was quite a large area of vegetable garden at the back.

"Nice and spacious, and a good suntrap too!" said Sarah, happily.

The manager stayed by the backdoor for a moment and started speaking to someone.

"Oh, right, Llanblodwel, eh? Where? Ok, Llynclys Hill, that's on the...right, the A495, turn right and it's at the furthest point along that road."

"I thought he might have been arranging to meet his girlfriend on his mobile, but seems to be another property, I think," whispered Sarah.

"Yes Sarah, another haven for you to choose from!" said Alyssia quietly, "but it's not a mobile, it's a Bluetooth device!"

"Oh, one of those earpiece whatsits!" she replied.

The manager called over as he advanced towards Sarah and Alyssia.

"Ladies! There's another property come up. It's over to the east of Llanblodwel as you may have heard. Would you like to see it?" he asked.

"Yes, although I like this place very much, I might as well see Blodwel's barn on the way back," replied Sarah, and the manager smiled.

The Ferrari doubled back past the crossroads and T-junction, coming to a 'nicely wider B road' as Sarah had mentioned, which took them through Llanblodwel, joining the A road previously mentioned. Soon they made a right turn and drove up to the top of the lane.

"There's quite a lot of houses up this road," remarked Sarah.

"Handy of you want to borrow some sugar," responded the manager.

The little cottage at the top of the lane had a nice airy feeling, but the garden was a bit more open to the elements.

Back at the estate agents, Sarah said that the first cottage was the one she was most interested in, and wanted to revisit it in a day or two's time.

"Can I call you when I get back, to check on the best times?" queried Sarah.

"We've found a lovely treasure of a cottage near a crag!" announced Sarah at lunchtime, "just south of Llansilin."

"Is it lovely and basic too?" asked Kenny mischievously.

"I want you to come over and inspect it properly, and no flippancy required Mr Kenton!" admonished Sarah, jovially.

"Yes ma'am!" cried Kenny, saluting intently, "I shall be free to come tomorrow afternoon as Bertha is coming to do her shop-sitting!"

"Oh good. I'll phone the estate agents and get the key from them," said Sarah.

Alyssia looked a bit preoccupied, and wasn't joining in with the conversation.

"Alyssia!" cried Karin, "are you all right?"

Alyssia turned her head, but didn't seem to be looking at anyone directly.

"All I can see are those bright lights and symbols again in front of my eyes. I can't concentrate on anything else," said Alyssia.

She got up as if to go somewhere, but moved uncertainly over towards the window, and bumped into a cupboard.

"Would someone help point me to my room, I'm getting dizzy!" she said.

Karin took her through, and sat on a chair by the bed as Alyssia settled herself, disappearing under the covers.

"I'll make you some herbal tea, Alyssia," said Karin, and was about to get up, but Alyssia restrained her by reaching for her arm.

"Stay! I need to know what this means. I want to record what is going on. Can you find a mauve notebook, there's one on the top shelf, I think," said Alyssia.

Karin quickly found it and sat by Alyssia again, poised and ready to write.

"Can I write anything down, Alyssia?" she asked.

Alyssia's face looked disorientated and then she spoke.

"Karin, I think I must just concentrate for now!" she said.

Karen got up to leave, "Just shout if you want me to return," she said, looking back to see Alyssia's closing eyes and an expression of inner concentration.

"She's just lying on the bed. There's not much we can do, is there?" asked Karin, looking around at Sarah and Kenny.

"If only we could make sense of it," commented Sarah.

"I wonder if it could be time to go back and visit Anchorin, and see if he knows anything," said Kenny, "I'd go now, but duty calls until five pm."

"Perhaps I should go, since you two are working," said Sarah, "but is the therapy room free?" and she looked at Kenny.

"Sorry, Sandra's doing some massaging this afternoon," said Kenny, glumly.

"A five o'clock wait it is!" replied Sarah, "well, we can take it in turns watch over Alyssia."

"Yes, Sarah, I'd better finish these letters as they need posting today," said Karin, getting up to return to her desk.

"I'll see you later, time to open the shop again," said Kenny, heading for the flat door.

Sarah cleared the table and did the washing up. A cry came from Alyssia's room. Sarah and Karin looked at each other, and Sarah swiftly went to her room.

"Alyssia, what's happening?" asked Sarah.

"This light, it's blinding me," said Alyssia, "I can't see anything, and it's beginning to hurt my eyes."

"I wish there was something we could use," said Sarah.

An impression of green powder came into her mind.

"I've got it!" cried Sarah, "I've got the impression to use the green powder of the elixir plant. I'll go and get some pronto, Alyssia!"

Sarah ran to the kitchen, shouting to Karin, "Karin! Where's the elixir potion? We need to give it to Alyssia."

Karin rushed to the cupboard where they kept all the tinctures and plant seed supplies, and opened it.

"There's some here, Sarah, and it's diluted!" replied Karin.

She quickly gave it to Sarah, who ran back to Alyssia's side.

"Alyssia, here's some elixir potion, can you sit up and take a mouthful? It should work!" said Sarah.

"But I'll get bigger!" exclaimed Alyssia.

"I'm just following intuition. At least try it," encouraged Sarah.

Alyssia took a mouthful, then two more, and then lay back again, still looking dazed. She appeared to be growing a little in size, as would usually happen, but then the growing

64

stopped after about a foot. After ten minutes of watching Alyssia, Sarah noticed that she had gone to sleep. Sarah then went back to the living room.

"It's calmed things down, Karin. Alyssia's gone to sleep now," said Sarah.

"Oh I'm so glad to hear that, Sarah," said Karin, "shall we take it in turns to look in on her periodically?"

"All right then, Karin," responded Sarah, "until Kenny comes up."

"Then he can visit Anchorin," replied Karin.

Chapter 5 – Summoned to the Temple

The phone rang at about quarter to five, and Karin answered it.

"We have a visitor, Karin, a Mr Ben Hudd!" said Kenny, cheerfully.

Karin simultaneously received the telepathic message that it was Hudlath."

"Oh, lovely!" responded Karin, "would he like to come upstairs?"

"Yes, he wishes to do so, just come down and escort him up," replied Kenny.

Karin put the phone down and excitedly turned to Sarah.

"It's Hudlath, Sarah! He's just arrived in the shop! I'll go and bring him up," cried Karin.

"Oh great, hurrah!" cried Sarah, with a beaming smile, "I'll go and check Alyssia again."

The familiar figure of Hudlath was there by the counter, with his long, white, shoulder length hair, and beard. He had donned his usual bright green velvet jacket for travelling in modern times.

"Hello! Hello! Karin," he said cheerfully, and his eyes appeared luminous, fresh from a golden age Atlantean environment.

"Lovely to see you Hudl..er, Mr Hudd!" replied Karin, "come upstairs! See you shortly, Kenny."

"Yes, I hope for some serious buyers to justify my having to wait down here meanwhile!" said Kenny telepathically, and "see you later!" he said out loud.

Once in the flat, Hudlath indicated immediately why he was there.

"Hello Sarah!" and he gave her and Karin a pat on their shoulders.

"Girls, I've come to see Alyssia," he explained, "there's a strong connection between her and Maraya and I need to find out why, as I think it's a clue as to Maraya's whereabouts."

"I've just been to see her, she's lying down in her bedroom, Hudlath," commented Sarah, and she explained everything that had happened with Alyssia, and giving her the elixir tincture.

"That's right, best thing to have done, Sarah," answered Hudlath, "do you know exactly what it was that started this off?"

"The dolphin's communication with her on Old Oswestry hill fort, Hudlath," responded Sarah.

"I know it is on a ley line, and an important energy site, but from a dolphin, and there's more!" explained Hudlath, "it's messages and energy coming from the Pleiades, do you know that?" and the others nodded, "the thing is that it can be very powerful, and comes as intuitive impressions rather than linguistically, so, on the physical level it is not easily understood. If she were given more elixir plant, she'd manage to grasp it, as well as amaranth. I don't know what she received, so I am unable to tell you. But if I took her back to Anchorin's temple, then we could download, as you say in these times, to access what is stored inside her mind."

"Will she be able to get up soon, Hudlath?" asked Sarah.

"I'll go through and give her some healing, if you can prepare some more of the potions," said Hudlath.

"Alyssia, it's Hudlath," he said reassuringly, as she lay slumbering, "I'm just going to give you some crystal healing, so just lie there, you don't need to move at all."

He brought out a crystal wand of a deep azure colour, and another clear quartz one, and began to work up and down Alyssia until there was a bright glow around her. Her aura was filled with the azure hue and a bright white light surrounded that.

Sarah came through with the potions.

"Do you want them together in the same glass, Hudlath?" she asked.

"Yes Sarah, that will be fine, she'll probably stir in a moment," responded Hudlath, and he put his crystal wands away in his shoulder bag. Alyssia opened her eyes and looked around.

"Sarah! Oh it's Hudlath!" and she looked astonished and gleeful.

Hudlath grinned widely, "yes, it's me all right! I've just given you an Atlantean healing, which has balanced you up!"

"What about those strange images I saw, what does it all mean?" asked Alyssia, looking preoccupied again.

"We'll go back to Anchorin's temple and then we'll see from there," explained Hudlath, "that's the best thing to do. Anyway, it's potion time!"

He took the glass offered by Sarah and gave it to Alyssia, and she drank it.

"Oh, I'm growing a little again," remarked Alyssia.

"Don't worry, it will soon wear off, it's only giving you some bodily strength to withstand what you've experienced," explained Hudlath.

Karin came through with Kenny.

"How is she?" Karin asked.

"Fine now, just fine! I think a nice meal will do her the world of good!" said Hudlath.

"I'll make it!" insisted Sarah, "I'm in the mood for cooking right now. It's most unusual, so take advantage of it while it lasts!" and she marched out purposefully.

"Thanks, Sarah, that's lovely," said Kenny, "feeling a bit better now, Alyssia?"

"I just feel tired, but generally fine," replied Alyssia.

"I'm sure we'll be able to take you to Anchorin's tomorrow morning," said Hudlath.

"Yes, I'd go sooner if I could," said Alyssia.

"Tomorrow will be fine," insisted Hudlath.

"We'll wake you again when the tea's ready, if you wish to continue sleeping, Alyssia," said Karin.

"Thank you, I think I will," said Alyssia sleepily, and she lay on her side facing the door, and was asleep again before the others had reached the living room.

"You know that there are further links between the dolphins and sea temples?" asked Hudlath.

"If dolphins are Pleiadean," ventured Sarah, "then perhaps the link with that planet was being perpetuated."

"Yes indeed," replied Hudlath, "and the important point is that only certain high priests and priestesses could interpret that wordless language that Alyssia received."

"Why did she receive it?" asked Kenny.

"Because in times past, she would have known it, but now she has forgotten the skill. Also, she isn't Atlantean sized, and our food is of a much higher quality, both of which enhances stamina at all levels."

"Where do you think Maraya's gone, Hudlath?" asked Kenny curiously.

"It's still a puzzle. When I saw an image of her in my crystal, she looked happy, but of course, Alyssia's face came up, so I began thinking of the possible connections between them, and by that time Maraya's face had faded," explained Hudlath, "I've yet to travel back further in time to check on that vortex and see what's happening. We can't have rogue vortices sucking people off like that, can we?"

"Certainly not, Hudlath, but could we help?" asked Karin.

"If either of you two would like to scout around and see where the vortex originates, that would be helpful," responded Hudlath, "in fact, it could be done from the mainland, while keeping contact with the sea temple, to maintain your safety. I'm sure you could see what the vortex was doing from there, since it would be pretty huge by then."

"Yes, we'll do it, won't we Karin!" exclaimed Sarah.

"Certainly, when would you like us to go, Hudlath?" asked Karin.

"As soon as you can possibly manage," said Hudlath, "I'll give you an explanatory letter to give to Zalarin at the sea temple."

Hudlath extracted his crystal from his shoulder bag, pointed it towards the bag and uttered something under his breath, then reached inside and produced the letter.

"Here you are!" he said, to a group of astonished faces.

"I feel a bit left out, folks!" said Kenny resignedly, "but someone has to be dutiful and mind the shop!" and he adopted a purposeful look.

"I'm sure your help will be required at some point, Kenny, it usually is!" remarked Hudlath, with a twinkle in his eye.

"Yes, I need a bit of the adventurous life too!" Kenny retorted, and Hudlath chuckled.

Next morning everyone was having breakfast around the living room table.

"What time will the healing room be occupied this morning, Kenny?" asked Hudlath.

"Oh! There's a client coming into the healing room around nine o'clock, Hudlath," replied Kenny.

"We don't want to draw attention to ourselves dressed in Atlantean clothing!" said Hudlath.

"Perhaps we should start selling some as the ultimate New Age fashion line, to detract attention?" suggested Kenny.

"You may have a point there, Kenny!" laughed Hudlath.

"I'll work on it! I'll have to open the shop in fifteen minutes!" replied Kenny.

"Time we made a quick exit!" responded Hudlath.

Hudlath and Alyssia got up, said goodbye to everyone and they departed to Anchorin's temple. Kenny was now downstairs in the shop, checking around to ensure everything was ready in time. He opened the healing room door just to see an aura of silvery turquoise light where the two had departed, and it was now fading.

'Good! I wouldn't want Sandra to start asking awkward questions!' thought Kenny.

Upstairs, Karin was talking to a customer on the phone.

"I'll just slip to the estate agents Karin, and make that appointment to see the house," said Sarah.

She went to open the flat door quietly, so as to not disturb Karin, but then Karin spun round in her office chair and handed Sarah a small shopping list, miming the word please. Sarah smiled and gave a thumbs up sign and left.

There stood the inspiring mountain where Anchorin's temple was perched at the summit. Hudlath and Alyssia walked slowly past Sarah's waterfall, and its energy cast a silvery aura, which radiated outwards across the valley. They could see the many fairies, and elves working hard to restore life above ground to its original state.

"I think the restoration team are almost finished the job, Alyssia," said Hudlath, cheerfully. He observed Alyssia closely, "your aura looks very tired, let's get a mountain buggy!"

He projected the thought mountainwards and a buggy appeared in front of them, and Hudlath guided Alyssia towards it.

"Ah good! Come in Alyssia! Hudlath! It's splendid to see you again, my friends!" cried Anchorin.

Anchorin's animated mien caused his violet eyes to become illuminated, and he put a protective arm around Alyssia, and the other around Hudlath and clapped him on the back.

"Let's get Alyssia to a healing chamber," he said.

He took Alyssia's arm, while Hudlath had the other, and they guided her into the temple.

Anchorin had obviously projected the thoughts to some of the priests for urgent assistance, as they began to appear swiftly, and he gave them further telepathic instructions. The three of them went into the healing chamber.

"Please make yourself comfortable on the crystal healing bed, Alyssia," said Anchorin.

They continued to guide her to it and she got on. Anchorin swiftly placed a silvery white blanket, which was made of a fleecy material and covered in minute crystalline particles. Anchorin adjusted a control box beside the bed, with wires connected to the end of the bed. Alyssia's body was lifted upwards slightly as a result, and remained hovering, while the amethyst and clear quartz crystals shone brightly. A priest came in and began to burn some herbs, producing a powerful aroma.

"What is that herb the priest's burning, Anchorin?" asked Alyssia, her speech was slow and slightly slurred.

"Ah, it's a combination of what we call the 'gift of sight plant', 'gifts of spirit plant' and some 'energy stronghold plant'," he replied.

"Quite similar to the effects of some of your plants your wise people use or used to use, but I can't be sure, as many of our plants didn't survive the end of Atlantis," commented Hudlath.

"We are going to link you in with our trusty equipment now, that will discover more about your information, Alyssia. The machine will take over with receiving all this instead of you now, but has to take them all from your mind first," explained Anchorin, "Uyindin! Can you please bring over the source machine," he looked at Alyssia again and spoke to her, "it means the machine that converts language coming from the source," he smiled sunnily.

Uyindin gently brought it over to place on a table by the crystal bed, and was level with it. Anchorin plugged it into the side of the bed and switched it on.

"This machine will begin to link into what you've been receiving very shortly," said Anchorin reassuringly.

Uyindin brought over a head cap and gave it to Anchorin.

"Alyssia, I am placing this cap on your head so we can begin the monitoring process," said Anchorin.

Anchorin had begun to speak louder as Alyssia's consciousness was beginning to drift, but she seemed to acknowledge what he'd said. The head cap was swiftly placed on Alyssia's head and the machine began whirring. Uyindin had attached the thin, turquoise wires, which connected to a large circular screen, and hung on the wall opposite the foot of Alyssia's healing bed.

Suddenly the screen lit up and sprung into action. The glyphs were etched in a radiant white light and flashed up on the screen as speedily as a computer identifying the contents of a large file.

"The velocity of this information! No wonder poor Alyssia's experiencing such a strain!" commented Anchorin.

The screen continued to flash up the information.

"It is all being saved now in the crystal banks," said Uyindin "as well as any new ones, which will be diverted there."

"Excellent! Then we can recall it all at a slower pace once it has finished," responded Hudlath.

"No, we can see them now Hudlath," commented Anchorin, "for we have a diverter switch, which can send some of the saved glyphs to another screen to study; that adjacent one will do," and Anchorin pointed to one in a nearby alcove.

They went round to the alcove and Anchorin activated the diverter with his crystal.

"I thought you'd have these in your time Hudlath," said Anchorin.

"We did, but our systems are much stronger now, they aren't compatible any more and no-one has managed to reproduce the technology due to an element which isn't available in our time," explained Hudlath.

"Is it lubidinum or erigonium?" asked Anchorin.

"Lubidinum, Anchorin. I didn't want to tell you because it is used quite a lot in your time, and if it is scarce in our time, it won't help matters," said Hudlath.

"You don't need to worry about that. Uyindin is skilled in ensuring its 'growth' as you might say, and can show you later," explained Anchorin.

"I don't know why that information wasn't passed on to our Age," remarked Hudlath with a curious look, "or did Uyindin come from another time period?" Hudlath gave Anchorin a pertinent stare.

"You're right of course!" admitted Anchorin, "he did have a previous lifetime when such a skill was commonly used, and had total recall."

Hudlath gave Anchorin another pertinent stare, "stop teasing me and let's get on with this!"

Anchorin smiled and activated the screen with his crystal, and the glyphs came through slowly as planned. They observed each glyph intently as they appeared. After about ten minutes Anchorin stopped the process temporarily.

"What do you think, Hudlath?" asked Anchorin.

"They are exceedingly powerful messages and link to a much higher consciousness than many on earth can handle, even in our golden age," replied Hudlath.

"Yes, I agree entirely. Some of them are codes for raising one's consciousness, but others are like pieces of information once the codes have done their activation," explained Anchorin.

72

"Yes," said Hudlath thoughtfully, "you're right; a group of codes come first, followed by the information, and then more codes and further information, and so on."

"Did any they mean anything to you at all, Hudlath?" asked Anchorin.

"Can we look at some of the codes which looked like they had hidden shapes inside them, near the beginning, but I think I'd need much more time to study them," replied Hudlath.

"I'll activate the machine again and go back to the beginning and you could tell me which ones suggested that," said Anchorin.

He pointed his crystal at the diverter, a small ganglion-like attachment between the end of the wire and the screen itself.

The glyphs came up again and they proceeded to look through them all. Hudlath told Anchorin to stop the machine when he recognised the relevant codes.

"This is one of them, Anchorin!" cried Hudlath, "look at the shapes in it!"

They both studied it closely, and their eyes became very brightly illuminated. They looked at each other and it was as if they both knew even without telepathic communication. They had realised that the information was a huge action of consciousness raising, required for anyone to reach the communication capacity of someone living in a very advanced environment.

"Which star systems do you suggest?" asked Anchorin.

"I know that it's from the Pleiades since the glyphs came to Alyssia via a dolphin," replied Hudlath.

"Well then, of course it is!" responded Anchorin, "it's time to call Zanadar! The glyphs I've seen at times were certainly not as powerful as these!"

Anchorin reached for his crystal and concentrated hard. After a moment there was a ping of light and Zanadar's face appeared.

"Greetings Anchorin! Ah, and Hudlath!" exclaimed Zanadar, "how can I help you?" and he beamed cheerfully.

"We have a concern here, Zanadar. Alyssia has been receiving masses of glyphs telepathically. They are proving too powerful for her to deal with. We have her here in this healing room half conscious, and although we have extracted all the ones in her memory, and diverted other ones that are still coming, but she is still very exhausted. What do you suggest?" asked Anchorin.

"Who or what gave her these glyphs?" asked Zanadar.

"Oh, I should have said, it was a dolphin which appeared through a portal," replied Anchorin.

"Ah! Then our Pleiadean friend Aurion needs to come too," said Zanadar, "we'll arrive shortly!"

His face faded, and Anchorin looked slightly relieved.

"Perhaps they will know what the glyphs mean, and if so, whether any of them are being repeated periodically, or should some glyphs have gone astray, whether we've missed the context of some vital information," remarked Hudlath.

"Good point my friend!" said Anchorin, and he walked over to Alyssia, "Alyssia! We have called Zanadar, and he's coming to help."

At the mention of Zanadar's name Alyssia's eyes showed a flicker of animation and then they closed again.

"I wonder why there's such a connection with Alyssia, that's what I'd like to know, even though Maraya and she have that link to ancient Atlantis," remarked Anchorin pensively.

"Have you checked the caskets recently?" suggested Hudlath; "after all, they should have become complete in themselves now."

"Goodness me! I should have thought of that, Hudlath!" exclaimed Anchorin.

"We've been so busy ensuring Atlantis had recuperated, and now Alyssia, to remember the obvious! I'll call Uyindin!" responded Anchorin.

Anchorin concentrated on linking with Uyindin, when a look of realisation crossed his face.

"I can sense that Zanadar and Salaron have arrived!" exclaimed Anchorin, "Uyindin! Can you bring the caskets through?"

Just then there was a knock at the door, and a priest announced the presence of Zanadar and Salaron. The door opened once Anchorin gave the affirmative.

"Welcome my friends! Come in!" exclaimed Anchorin warmly, "thank you Gandan!" he said to the priest, who smiled at Anchorin and swiftly departed.

Zanadar and Salaron entered, and the two high priests went to greet them. Then Hudlath swiftly brought them over to see Alyssia. Zanadar laid his hand on her head, and his orange-pink skinned face glowed. His hands also began to glow strongly, and a halo of light came from the hand on Alyssia's head and suffused its energy through her body. Salaron had been quietly talking with Anchorin and was standing beside Zanadar. He was of a smaller build, slender and graceful, with

74

large blue eyes. His skin had a bluish tinge, with a slight incandescent sheen.

"So the glyphs are all saved Anchorin, let's see them, my friend," said Salaron, eager to get started.

"Certainly," responded Anchorin, and he went to switch on the round screen he and Hudlath had looked at earlier, "if you'd like to come over Salaron, Zanadar!"

Anchorin gave a slightly questioning look to Zanadar as they approached, indicative of Alyssia's condition.

"She's fine and I know she will just sleep on for the rest of the day, and maybe tomorrow for a while. I'm sure she will be able to get up at some stage, but to just take it gently," explained Zanadar.

"Good! We're beginning to make some progress," said Anchorin.

There was another knock at the door.

"Enter please Uyindin! The caskets! Good, please put them on the centre table, thank you," said Anchorin.

Uyindin brought them over in a customary carrying box, usually used for storing crystals not in use. It was stoutly made of wood with brass coloured handles and a latch to fasten it. Uyindin set the box down and carefully brought out the caskets, and then departed with the box.

"My friends, here are the three caskets together, and they may help us with our task in hand," commented Anchorin.

Zanadar and Salaron looked round at the caskets, pausing in thought. They appeared to be focusing on them intently.

"Can you open the lids Anchorin, and then step back!" instructed Zanadar, "but we'll all sit beside Alyssia before you do so!"

"The caskets will link to this symbolic knowledge and translate the information for Atlanteans to understand," explained Salaron.

Everyone went to sit down and then Anchorin opened the casket lids, and swiftly retreated to his seat, and they all awaited the outcome.

A strange stillness enveloped everyone. Uyindin and Gandan had said afterwards that everyone in the temple had stopped what they were doing and just stood transfixed. Bright light came from each casket, shining upwards and then fountained down over everyone in the room. The energy then permeated the files where all the glyphs had been stored, and bright cascades of light were gently activated by the energy linked to each glyph. This process happened very swiftly. Anchorin

75

and Hudlath felt an enormous feeling of great joy overcome them, and their eyes positively glowed. Anchorin looked at Alyssia and he saw a slow smile spread across her face. He indicated this to Hudlath, and then they all knew about it and smiled in response.

The energy of stillness increased and the whole temple was completely still. Brilliant light filled the healing room and increased in strength and intensity. All of a sudden, after a period of time, which no one could recall the exact duration, a flurry of activity swept the energy from the glyphs out of the computer banks, and it sped into the three caskets. There was a harmonious chord, which resonated strongly, and echoed around the room. Hudlath pointed to each of the caskets, indicating that they were each giving out one of the chord's notes. The sound radiated outwards now in waves, and seems to be everywhere in the temple. Then it was as if every person and object in the room at least vibrated in response, and all gave out a sound or chord accordingly.
Hudlath and Anchorin looked at each other, obviously quite moved by the beauty of all this sound. Zanadar and Salaron looked on with a glow of recognition to the others, indicating that they knew of such things already.

Chapter 6 – Ty Bach and the Atlantean Vortex

Sarah returned from the estate agents and entered the flat with a bag load of goodies.

"Here you are Karin!" exclaimed Sarah cheerfully, "more pick-me-up fodder for working women!"

Sarah put the bag on the living room table and extracted three packs of herbal tea from amongst the other groceries and placed them by the kettle.

"Did you get your appointment sorted out?" asked Karin.

"Yes, this afternoon, so Kenny can come," replied Sarah, putting the rest of the groceries away.

"Oh good, and then we can go to Atlantis after the shop closes and investigate that portal," replied Karin.

"Why don't we take a camera and get it on record?" suggested Sarah.

"Yes, why not, it would show something definite for Hudlath to examine," replied Karin, still busily working at her desk.

"What an enchanting little cottage, Sarah," said Kenny enthusiastically as they pulled up in Sarah's car that afternoon.

"I knew I had to get this cottage. Something's 'in the air' as they say, and I feel that something's compelling me to get this place, right on this area of land!" replied Sarah.

Kenny gave an appreciative expression.

"Let's get in it then and find out what it is!" he replied, with a grin.

"Don't let me stop you!" retorted Sarah.

They got out of the car and through the front gate. Kenny peered in through the two front windows and eyed the roof and guttering, and then they went in through the front door. Kenny studied all the details of the interior closely in each room, and then they both went outside to look at the garden.

"It's really quite a sizeable space out here, with fruit trees and vegetable plots, I'll be happy to come and help you, and it would be great to get out as I miss not having a garden where we are," commented Kenny.

"That would be marvellous, Kenny. Special discount on vegetables available!" and Sarah laughed.

"It's a deal. We'll be quids in!" and Kenny laughed too.

They wandered around the garden some more, looking to see what varieties of fruits and vegetables there were.

"There's a curiously overgrown area in this corner amongst the trees, Kenny!" exclaimed Sarah, "come and see!"

Kenny, who had been back over to the cottage to examine the guttering at the back, exterior walls and window frames, half ran over to where Sarah stood, by a gnarled old ash tree. Sarah pushed through some of the dense undergrowth.

"There appears to be water under here," said Sarah.

Kenny helped to part more of the grasses and removed some old oak branches, and placed them outside the treed area.

"It's a well, Sarah!" gasped Kenny, "it's lovely! Look! I can see some inscriptions on it!"

What they could see beneath the undergrowth was a circular basin, into which water bubbled upwards from the field behind the garden.

"My goodness!" cried Sarah, looking at Kenny in amazement, "they are strange! Not a language I know. If only I'd brought some paper, I could have written the symbols down," and Sarah was now searching her bag for any scraps of paper.

"Sorry, I don't have any myself," replied Kenny.

"Oh good, I've got a receipt, luckily there's no printing on the back, I'll try and cram what I can on it!"

Sarah kneeled, looking at the glyphs more closely. The basin was a very pale turquoise green, not the usual coppery verdigris but a ceramic glaze with a sparkling glint to it. The symbols had been applied afterwards somehow, and had a burnt gold tinge to them. Sarah ran her hand gently over the first symbol thoughtfully, and then stood up. She had to peer through the undergrowth to see each of them, and she began reading the symbols and copied them one by one onto the back of the receipt.

"Well, this is intriguing!" commented Sarah, "let's get back so I can get that contract signed, eh Kenny!"

"Good thinking!" replied Kenny, folding the undergrowth back over the basin, "I'm wanting to get that corner cleared up!"

They returned to the car swiftly and drove back to Oswestry.

"Was there much at fault Kenny?" Sarah asked when they had been in the car.

"Nothing too serious," Kenny had replied, "just a bit of routine maintenance which I could fix easily. For instance, one or two brackets on the guttering need fixing, a bit of plastering around some bathroom tiles, and so on, no problem about that!"

"Good, I'm so glad the house is in good order, almost!" said Karin, happily, "while you were out a huge order delivery arrived and the delivery man kindly helped me get them in."

"Yes, I wondered why I could only get up the stairs sideways!" remarked Kenny.

"Oh well, duty calls!" said Sarah, "I don't think we'll have the energy to go to Atlantis tonight with all that!" and they looked at each other.

"Right then!" said Kenny, "we'll have to open them up, check 'em off as usual and stock up the shop. Let's get started then!"

They all brought batches of the boxes up into the flat to begin work.

A silvery green landscape stretched to the horizon. Sarah walked slowly over it, looking around her. The grass under her feet was soft and inviting, and she could feel her feet tingling with energy. 'Just as you'd expect on a ley line or power point,' thought Sarah.

There in front of her appeared a wood.

'Oh, I didn't notice that before! It appeared very suddenly!' she thought, 'lovely oak trees though.'

As she approached the wood, there was a spring green mist that emanated from the ground, and a perfume wafted towards her.

'That smell! Why does it remind me of something, yet I don't know what it is!' she thought, 'slightly like cedarwood, mixed with frangipani!'

She felt hands on her shoulders, gently guiding her into the wood. Although the wood wasn't very big, it was as if the location was suddenly enormous once she entered. No sign of any boundaries were visible, and that the wood stretched in all directions for miles.

'This wood reminds me of the inside of the Tardis, dimension-wise!' thought Sarah.

"Come forward and do not be afraid!" were the impressions Sarah received just then.

She replied in the affirmative and walked onwards, and came to a small pond.

"Step into the water," came another impression.

Sarah looked around her, but saw no one. She put her foot out to step forwards and the pond began to effervesce with light. She stood into it and the pond expanded until it was about twenty feet wide and circular. Pure crystalline water poured into the pond, bubbling up like a spring from the centre. Sarah expected she'd get wet, but the water felt only to be like a mist swirling around her. She looked around the edges and saw symbols surrounding it, and realised with a jolt that they were the glyphs on her pond at Ty Bach, and they were beginning to glow with a light of their own.

"What does it mean?" she cried out.

"You will know when you go to live there," came the reply.

Sarah woke suddenly and she looked at her clock, it was only 7.30am. She lay there recalling her dream.

'I shall tell the others all about it, yet I still don't know what the symbols mean!' she thought.

At breakfast Sarah retold her dream to Karin and Kenny.

"Very curious!" said Karin.

"I really can't wait until you move in!" replied Kenny; "we'll just have to scry with our Atlantean crystals until then!"

"We can look at your symbols meanwhile, Sarah," said Karin.

"Yes, I'd better start writing them out properly, while I still remember how they really looked," said Sarah, "could I have some of your office paper? and I'll get the all-important receipt!"

Sarah began sketching out the symbols as she remembered them, whilst using the receipt as reference. She did two on every sheet of paper and handed the first one to Karin, who looked at them carefully. Kenny took the next sheet just offered.

"They're amazing, Sarah! Who on earth lived there before, did the estate agent know?" asked Karin, curiously.

"It must have been the brother of old eccentric Emrys the alchemist from Cwm Rheiddol valley!" retorted Kenny.

"Oh yes, him! Of course dear!" replied Karin, laughing.

"The estate agents didn't know any further back than two ownerships, both of whom have either passed away or moved house a few times," explained Sarah. "I did ask for details, with the pretence that I wanted to write a historical novel featuring Ty Bach. They also said that another estate agent had previously dealt with the cottage, and the present branch is in Shrewsbury," and she gave a shrug.

"Could be a bit tedious trying to find out," commented Kenny, "easier just to use our intuition, and with some help from our friends both here and in Atlantis. As was said, I'm sure the purpose will present itself."

"I expect you're right, Kenny, the thought of a full-scale investigation would curtail any enthusiasm," replied Sarah.

"How many symbols are there altogether, Sarah, have you finished writing them all out?" asked Karin.

"Yes, I have now," Sarah replied, removing the receipt from the table, tucking it into one of her pockets. There are seven, though whether they are letters or glyphs, I know not."

"Maybe glyphs to us, and letters to an unknown race," replied Karin thoughtfully.

"Seems outrageous to have an archaic sentence on a pool at the bottom of your garden," said Sarah, "and that no one knows anything about it! Do you think it could be of the elemental kingdom?"

"I really don't know! I'll have to get that shop open now, but when will you two get to Atlantis? Then you might find out the answer!" said Kenny.

"Yes Kenny, when is the room free downstairs?" asked Sarah.

"Booked until lunchtime, and then I think from 2pm. There's a slot of time over lunch, but make sure you leave me some sandwiches before you go!" teased Kenny, and he got up to leave.

"Yes dear!" replied Karin with a gracious air, "off you go and do your duty!"

"As long as you do yours!" smiled Kenny.

Karin looked at Sarah, and they gave affirmation with a thumbs up sign.

"See you later girls!" said Kenny, "will ring if I'm wrong on the therapy room times."

"I'll make another copy of these glyphs to take with us to Atlantis, and we can ask at the appropriate time, after we've checked the origins of the portal," said Sarah.

"Sandwiches for monsieur!" exclaimed Karin.

She put them on a plate, covered in a plastic bag, and left them on the living room table.

"Let's go Karin, it's 12.30! I can't wait to return to Atlantis," said Sarah happily, grabbing her camera and putting it in her backpack.

They went down the staircase that led to both the shop and outer doors, and also to an outer door of the healing room, which they entered. They found their Atlantean clothes in a corner cupboard, and then took their elixirs, expanding to twelve feet high.

"Where shall we concentrate on? Anchorin's temple or Chalidocea?" asked Karin.

"How about near the entrance to the main temple in Chalidocea?" suggested Sarah; "I don't suppose it would bother them about people popping up out of the blue. After all, Hudlath does it all the time!"

"Ok, we need to get going!" said Karin.

"Chalidocean temple 12,000 BC!" said Sarah.

Sarah and Karin both held their crystals and concentrated on that time period, and in a flash they had disappeared. There was a blur of colour and they reappeared outside the temple.

"A buggy will take us out to Zalarin's temple, lets look out for one!" said Sarah.

They wandered off down the main street, which would lead them northwards along the street called the Summer Islands Way, which would reach the exit to the city at the Summer Islands Gate. Soon they could hear a buggy's familiar low, gentle humming sound a street or two away and the sound was getting gradually louder. They turned to look and saw it approaching from one of the side roads behind the temple.

"Would you take us to Zalarin's temple please?" asked Karin telepathically.

The buggy driver nodded and replied in the same way.

"Yes, it will be a pleasure. Do get in," he said, and they set off.

They waved cheerfully to the departing buggy driver when they arrived. They were now standing where the path led down the incline to the beach, and where they would continue onwards towards Zalarin's sea temple shortly.

"Those mountains of the old continent are grander than I thought," said Karin, staring intently at them.

"Yes, it's a curiously attractive place," remarked Sarah thoughtfully, "even though we are a fair distance away, there's a strange atmosphere about it that I can't explain at present."

"Yes, you're right Sarah," replied Karin, "but it holds more of an atmosphere of intrigue than anything else to me."

They walked swiftly along the beach path to the temple, asked for Zalarin and handed him Hudlath's letter to look at.

"Good! If you need the sea vessel, it is over there by the water's edge, and it just needs a crystal to operate it, no doubt you have one to spare, since you've travelled with them?" queried Zalarin.

"We do Zalarin, but can we travel from here?" asked Sarah, "We understand that we'll start off from where Hudlath left off, which was when Elaharia was above water, near the end times."

"That's right!" agreed Zalarin, "8,400 years ago from now, that will show the vortex as covering all those mountains of the Summer Islands," he explained, indicating them with his arm outstretched.

A priest called out to Zalarin.

"Proceed as you wish, and you are welcome to contact me if you need to, farewell for now," he said.

He gave Sarah and Karin a friendly smile, handed the letter back, and then departed with a quick wave to walk over to the priest.

They pulled out their crystals and mentally visualised 8,400 years ago as the destination. The air shimmered brightly around them, and then once the time period established itself, they saw the northern continent a couple of miles away from where they stood, as before, except that the land had risen within the Summer Islands, and the rest of the continent was less than two miles away.

"That's a huge vortex, Sarah!" exclaimed Karin, "I've often wondered how big they can get!"

Sarah brought out her camera, focused and clicked.

"First one for the records, so we can compare with whatever comes next," commented Sarah.

"Shall we go back another 600 years?" asked Karin, "it's what Hudlath did initially."

"21,000BC! Okay, let's go then!" smiled Sarah.

They concentrated with their crystals again. The area around them shimmered once more and then settled into a similar view. The old sea temple nearby was still in use.

"I'm glad the sea temple's still being used, though it can't be the same sea vessel moored there!" smiled Karin.

"The vortex has grown a little wider, but nothing dramatic to see," remarked Sarah, "but I'll take another picture all the same."

Sarah produced her camera and took a shot.

"We'll have to go back much further, Sarah," said Karin.

"Right! How about another 2,000 years or so, taking us to 23,400BC years ago, in total?" asked Sarah.

Karin agreed, and they travelled further back in time again. The vortex was a shimmering mass, stretching about one Atlantean mile or two statute miles across, well beyond the circular mountains.   Sarah's camera was out again and clicking.

"That image looks good, I'll just enlarge it to examine the details," said Sarah, as Karin came over to look.

"I can see something in the centre of it, perhaps we should ask the local priests here and see if they know of it," suggested Karin.

"I'll keep my camera out of sight in case they think we're on the prowl!" responded Sarah.

They cautiously approached the sea temple.   A priest appeared, and he looked at them intently.

"Who are you, please, and what are you here for?" he asked, telepathically.

"We have come back in time from Anchorin's time period and spoke to Zalarin, who was your sea temple's high priest in that time period as well. We wish to know more about the vortex over there, is your high priest knowledgeable?" asked Sarah.

"How do we know you are genuine?" the priest asked, with a pertinent look.

Sarah brought out the letter for Zalarin and then she noticed a list of names printed on the bottom of the page, with time periods next to them. Next to 23,000 BC was written, Keirion.

"Keirion is your high priest is he not?" enquired Sarah; "I have an introductory letter to Zalarin from Hudlath, another high priest.

"Please wait here by the entrance and I shall return with Keirion," he said and swiftly departed.

A broad shouldered man appeared, and his deep blue eyes and wide face echoed with strength, and they could see that spiritual strength was also reflected in his eyes.

"Who told you my name, my friends?" he asked.

"Hudlath, who comes from the time period 200 years after Anchorin's time," explained Sarah, "would you like to see his letter?"

"No!" said Keirion, holding up his hand to stop Sarah from handing her letter to him, "I'll contact him myself and find out for sure."

He brought out his crystal and focused on it. After a moment, Hudlath's face appeared.

"Ha! Keirion, how can I be of service, my friend?" asked Hudlath.

"I have two ladies called....?" And he looked at them inquiringly.

"Sarah and Karin," replied Sarah.

"Yes! As I would expect! That's why I made a list of high priests' names on the letter! Any problems?" enquired Hudlath.

"I just wanted to be sure who they were, as we very occasionally get island folk coming over, and not all with good intentions," explained Keirion.

"Do they look suspicious? You always were a stickler for detail!" retorted Hudlath.

"Yes, alright Hudlath. All is well now. Goodbye my friend," replied Keirion, and his face broke into a sunny smile. "I'm sorry, my friends, come on in!"

They followed Keirion to his office and they sat down and explained what they were looking for and why.

"I see," said Keirion with a serious look, and he pondered in thought a moment, "and in the centre of that vortex is what is called a light-year portal in your language, as Hudlath informed me would be a term you'd understand. This is where anyone can travel through, not only time, but across galaxies, and perhaps, as some say, via that to other universes."

"How did the portal get created?" asked Karin.

"It was made by the people of the Pleiades, so that they could oversee how humanity was progressing on this planet, since it was an experiment for them to integrate some races of theirs onto your planet and oversee their progress, as you know. They needed to monitor the planet from afar, from their own domain," explained Keirion. "So an instability encroached on the vortex after the whole time travel vortices had been re-opened and so on? I'll contact my high priest friend from Galaron, Lemuria, concerning Elaharia district and see what he says. You don't need to ask him any questions as he instantly knows them!"

Keirion produced his crystal again, focussing intently. A face with a white beard appeared over the crystal. Keirion explained his reason for calling him, and indicated the presence of his guests beside him.

"Greetings to you!" said the high priest, looking around at Sarah and Karin, "my name is Galaron, and I am strongly linked to the Pleiadeans via my ancestors.

85

He looked at them intently, and light shone from his eyes with a beautiful and unearthly radiance, and they looked visibly moved.

Galaron continued, "it is true about the light-year portal, which has been on Atlantis since the beginning, when the Pleiadean peoples initially lived here. Despite the dark forces, which periodically ravage our planet, we have kept it going. I am pondering on the cause of why the portal is now behaving strangely, because, at the end of our civilisation when we knew that our beloved land would be about to perish, we deliberately planned to close the whole portal, and the light-year portal was closed 2,000 years later than our present period," here, Galaron paused in thought.

"Is there any way we could either seal it up altogether, or ensure it only is opened when a high priest who is qualified to operate it, is present," ventured Keirion.

"Yes indeed, I shall have to close it firmly, and then open it again. But, as you say, to ensure that it is only open in the time periods when suitably qualified high priests are around," said Galaron, "that should sort it out."

"But we must know where our friend Maraya has gone to, before doing anything," said Sarah, with concern.

"Don't worry, I shall ask our Pleiadean friends to help, and I shall travel along and see where she is. Leave it to me!" said Galaron, reassuringly, "I won't be longer than a day or two, Keirion."

"Thank you Galaron, my friend," replied Keirion.

Galaron's smiling face disappeared, and Keirion put his crystal away.

"You are welcome to rest here, and join in with our temple activities and our life in general. There's plant rearing, herbal medicine making, arts and crafts, and our ceremonies outdoors that happen with the setting sun. I'll show you to a room you can use," he explained, and rose from his seat.

"There's one thing I'd like to ask, Keirion, if it is right to do so," ventured Sarah.

Keirion stopped in his tracks and looked at Sarah intently.

"It's about Galaron and his Pleiadean ancestry," she said.

Keirion immediately understood, and Sarah didn't need to elaborate any further.

"Yes, you may well wonder! And why no one else around is quite the same. Apparently Galaron was one of the first people on Atlantis, having also lived on Lemuria, and he was the offspring of one of those Pleiadeans. Despite being born on Earth, he strongly wished to return to the Pleiades to understand his origins, but he liked it so much there, that he didn't want to return. Pleiadeans can live on their world for hundreds of years. He was advised by elders, however, to return, and he also took the unusual step of wanting to ensure perpetuation of the Pleiadean link and knowledge by travelling forward in time from the first Golden Age on Atlantis, which only people in the fifth dimension know how, and live for a while in our time now, that is immersed in the most material age, to ensure the knowledge would survive the continent's submergence, and be preserved in the Golden Age to come subsequently."

"Did he know about the three caskets that Anchorin has?" asked Karin.

"He originally compiled them, and if any difficulties on earth would arise, he'd ensure the caskets and many other important documents went into the portal, and would lock it shut until danger passed," explained Keirion, "though the caskets' disappearance began to happen in our time, and all of them had gone by the end of Atlantis. However, for centuries they existed only on the fifth dimension, and more as a vision than anything palpable in three dimensions. Their strength and depth of purpose have only became apparent since they were physically recovered and returned to Atlantis."

"Ah, I see!" responded Sarah.

"That explains a lot! Thank you Keirion," remarked Karin.

Galaron concentrated hard, looking deeply into the vortex with his depth of vision. Linking to this was easily done, for he was almost of the divine Pleiadean stock who first came to Earth all those centuries ago. They left a lasting legacy to humanity who would gradually learn to seek the divine source for themselves. In less than a moment, his vision expanded to encompass all potential destinations to which this vortex could lead him. He sought Maraya's image in his mind, which he could do, for the thought image of her was visible around Karin and Sarah when he looked intently towards them.

He slipped out of his body as it lay on his bed, and reached upwards and along star routes used in his time. He knew of Zanadar and the Council of Twelve from knowing Anchorin, but they were not of his time, for there were other Pleiadean, Sirian, and other galactic members who patrolled the heavens then. He contacted them as he searched, asking them to scour star systems for her presence. Their kindly affirmations linked to his mind as he searched. He knew that if he would travel in person, and the vortex was flawed, he could be left stranded somewhere, in the same way Maraya had been, apparently. He looked on outwards across the threshold of the solar system, pondering thoughtfully, whilst observing the increasingly smaller sized asteroids and Pluto-sized planets that orbited the extremities.

In the spirit world and from the fifth dimension upwards, all of space isn't dark, but a pale warm-toned sea-green hue. The planets hang, brightly glistening in the aura of radiant light put out by all the suns of solar systems, galaxies, and the god or goddess energy of the whole universe combined. The star route was a silver sparkling column through space that the vortex usually took, travelled past the nearest star group called the Pylon of Phairos. Galaron sped over to visit these stars. Planets around them held life, not as Earth knows it, but peopled by forms of higher dimensions, utilising the planets to build domes and structures of light to live and work inside. He sped past, sensing Maraya wasn't there.

"Orion is the next star system on the horizon and there are countless planets to be found there. Some are fourth dimensional, others fifth and in some places, sixth. As he approached Rigel's array of diaphanous planets of pearly light, he was met by the angelic-like beings from one or two of the planets. They always looked spectacular, with a brilliant iridescent cascade of energy emanating from them, and although they were human in shape, the brilliance of their auras made it difficult to see their features.

"Greetings fair spirit! Are you seeking something?" asked one being, telepathically as ever, though not verbally, but as an intuitive flash of knowing to Galaron.

"I'm looking for someone called Maraya," and he projected an image of Maraya as her dark-haired self, and also indicated her former life as the fair-haired high priestess. "Our vortices had been closed in order to halt the passage of Renegades filtering through from the End Times, and we took the Essence from the 'Garden of Eden' to help in this matter. It produced a permanent winter and no contact outside one's time period for a while. Once opened again, the problems started," explained Galaron.

The beings looked concerned and glanced at each other, which Galaron sensed, due to not being able to see them easily.

Galaron could see a force of energy passing between their foreheads, and after a moment they replied.

"We know of planets where this was necessary, and the shutting and opening of vortices can be very tricky, and should be done in stages. By use of some of the essence at each vortex, this will allow the frequencies to gain purity and strength again," they explained.

"But in this case, a vortex near my Elaharian temple in my time, where I am high priest, became re-opened 11,000 years later, and was responsible for this," replied Galaron, "that in itself seems unexceptional, but due to the fact that our continent sank 3,000 years after my time, and it was known in my time that it would happen. So we laid down a rule that when the time was nearly imminent, the rest of the vortex would be closed completely, for it would serve no further purpose. This re-opening procedure can obviously override any closure; but we must find out where Maraya went, and if she disappeared somewhere off the vortex's star-way."

"We have been re-telling your story to our colleagues all around the Orion star system as you've been communing. Are you travelling further on?" they asked.

"Yes, I am going to the Pleiades!" replied Galaron.

"Then we will send any thoughts of worth to you there, or visit you later on Earth when you return," they replied.

Galaron smiled gratefully and turned to move away.

"We understand Maraya needs to be found before the vortex can be dealt with in your time and then sealed up again near the end of your continent's lifespan," they concluded.

Galaron waved to the beautifully sparkling beings, and left.

Orion's chain of outer stars were visible to Galaron, but he sped past so fast that they became a blur. Beyond him, the biggest of the sun's, which was vast compared with Earth's sun, lit the heavens from afar, and it was fast becoming apparent to Galaron as he proceeded. The light was a bright blue-white brilliance, which would have blinded anyone in a physical body, but in his spirit body, although very bright, it didn't bother him.

'It's my torch to guide me homewards,' he thought, and was the usual phrase that came to mind on seeing it. He was, of course, approaching the constellation of Taurus, and would see the planetary group of Elara shortly, and their roseate glow would become visible.

'There!' he thought, 'the stepping stones to the final destination,' and he smiled.

Beings of light from the outer planet beckoned to him, he waved back, and sped over to them.

"Greetings! I am searching for my friend Maraya," said Galaron, and he retold the story to them as well.

Their delicate rose coloured features glowed brightly, with sparkles of gold floating around their energy fields, which dimmed a tiny fraction on hearing about Maraya.

"I am Caelina," said one of the beings, "this vortex!"

She had her back to the Pleiades, and silently stretched out her left arm and pointed downwards diagonally, and the other beings nodded.

"This is another star-way vortex that now crosses yours. It used to be completely separate, but has now become linked up with it since your re-opening. That is why it has caused the difficulties, and must be separated," explained Caelina.

"Will closure and re-opening it solve the problem?" asked Galaron.

"No, unfortunately," she replied, "the other star-way has to be disentangled by dissolving the part of it that is attached. There are many Pleiadeans who could help."

"Where does it start and end?" asked Galaron.

"It starts in the constellation of Auriga, near the star Capella, and runs down towards the sun of Achernar, to a small planet called Pelucia. It's in the constellation of Eridanus," the others chorused.

"Eridanus!" exclaimed Galaron, "that's so far off, and such a long star-way! If she's out there, I'm not sure how I can get her back that easily."

"We'll have to get the Council of Twelve to start scouting," said Caelina, "I'll contact Zarhavar while you return, and will get him to contact you," said Caelina.

"Would you be able to inform every planet you can?" asked Galaron.

"We shall indeed. We are familiar with this star-way to Pelucia, of course, as you are, but knew there was still a reason to keep it open," said Alayah, another of the beings.

"We don't know why there should be a problem for Maraya's return, once whatever is retaining her is lifted, and then re-enter your star-way vortex," remarked Caelina.

Galaron looked thoughtfully, "I've told the beings from the Rigel planets, could you tell them what we've found so far, and I'll return and see what I can do, and will send word to you all as we progress."

They greeted each other with a parting wave, and Galaron sped away Earthwards, not wishing to draw anywhere near to that junction of the Pelucian star-way, even though he was out of his physical body.

Sarah and Karin were immersed in helping in the herb garden presently, collecting a batch of herbs for the community's evening ceremony, and had been at work for much of the day.

"Thank you for your help," said a priestess, who wore the customary long garments like Sarah and Karin were wearing, "it is always good to have extra hands on manual work," and she smiled, wiping her forehead with the back of her hand, as her fingers had soil on them.

"Shall we take these herbs inside?" asked Sarah.

"No thank you, could you please just leave them in our ceremonial pot by the door over there," she replied.

She pointed to a small side door to the sea temple, and sure enough, a sturdy rounded pot of baked clay stood beside it. They took the herbs over, and Sarah lifted the lid while Karin placed them inside the dampened pot, to keep them fresh until the ceremony. They returned to the temple and went to their room to refresh themselves.

There was a knock on their door, and Karin and Sarah looked at each other.

"It's Keirion with some useful news I hope," said Karin, and Sarah expressed hopeful anticipation.

They opened the door to see Keirion's broad, strong figure standing there.

"Would you like to follow me to my office, we can talk there," he said.

"You see how complicated it could be," said Keirion, seriously.

"Yes indeed, will the Council of Twelve be able to rescue Maraya if she's there?" asked Karin.

"They would only be able to get to Pelucia, but with it being a fourth dimensional world, it is still not elevated enough for them to land on it, and also because it has not experienced a golden age either," explained Keirion, "but they could take people over to the edge of Pelucia's atmosphere, and those concerned could travel from there."

"Which people would be able to enter Pelucia's atmosphere?" asked Sarah, who glanced anxiously at Karin.

"Any Atlantean could manage, but they would need some form of antiviral substance, a very strong herbal mixture course taken over at least two days before going," recommended Keirion.

"I get a funny feeling that we will be going, somehow," said Sarah rather reluctantly.

"Yes, we know you are suited, since Hudlath told me of your venture to Colony B to rescue others in the past," replied Keirion, "of course, the Council of Twelve will sort out the necessary details, and I know Hudlath would travel with you again."

"We'll have to inform Costillo," said Sarah, "he is Maraya's partner, and lives in Anchorin's time."

"Oh indeed," remarked Keirion with a surprised look, "will you mind doing that?"

"Yes, we'll talk to Hudlath," replied Sarah.

"Why don't we tell Anchorin before we return, then he can pass the information on to all concerned, and we can see how Alyssia is too," suggested Karin.

"Why not!" agreed Sarah.

Keirion looked inquisitively at the mention of Alyssia's name, and Sarah explained about her condition.

"I think we have concluded for now, haven't we?" said Keirion, "I must prepare for our evening ceremony, will you join us?"

"Thank you for your kind invitation," said Sarah, "but we have to visit Anchorin, and after that, return to our own time."

"Yes, thanks, I'll have work to do too, once we return!" added Karin.

"It's going to be a long day for you both! Well, you'd better get going!" chuckled Keirion.

They said farewell and left the sea temple. With the usual time travel shimmering, Karin and Sarah were back in Anchorin's time. Karin used her crystal to call for a hoverbuggy.

The familiar sight of the main temple of Chalidocea came into full view. Its almost copper coloured oricalchum dome reflected brightly in the evening sun, and had been visible from the city's Summer Islands gateway. They passed it by and continued towards the Mountain Temple gateway. As they were approaching it, another buggy came towards them swiftly and stopped.

"Hi! Come on!" shouted a familiar figure.

"Hudlath! We're just coming to the temple," Sarah shouted back.

"Get on! I'll take you!" he replied.

Karin and Sarah thanked the buggy driver and stepped on beside Hudlath.

They merely talked about non-confidential subjects until they got off at the mountain, and now could compare notes while they were walking up its slopes until the mountain buggy's arrival.

"Hudlath, we met the person who invented the caskets!" cried Karin.

"And as he travelled towards the Pleiades, a being told him that Maraya is being held on Pelucia. It is linked to a crossed vortex which needs untangling, but after rescuing Maraya!" exclaimed Sarah.

"Alright!" cried Hudlath with a smile, who'd been trying to get a word in edgeways! "Okay! It is all very encouraging. Let's start from the beginning, but you may wish to save your energy, as you'll need to explain it all in full when we get to Anchorin's temple. Perhaps you may wish to save the rest until then, eh!"

"Yes, I think so, but how about Alyssia? Is she better?" asked Karin earnestly.

"Yes, yes! No problem. Zanadar and Salaron helped, and she's fine. You'll find out everything when we get there, I can assure you," and he smiled happily.

Sarah and Karin positively ran towards the temple entrance, followed closely by Hudlath, gliding swiftly.

A priest showed them to the healing room where Alyssia was recuperating. Karin and Sarah smiled to see Alyssia sitting up and went to greet her. Anchorin was already present, with Zanadar and Salaron standing beside him. They smiled on seeing the entrants.

"Greetings!" cried Hudlath in the Atlantean customary manner.

He raised his forearm with palm facing forwards, the way American Indians would do; Anchorin, Zanadar and Salaron returned the greeting. They sat and exchanged details on everything that had happened.

"That's a fancy gadget you have there!" remarked Anchorin on seeing Sarah's digital camera.

"I took images of the vortex at different times," she said, quickly preparing it for viewing.

"I see it! The light year portal. Yes, that was closed a long time ago, when deemed too much like inviting trouble," commented Anchorin, "and you spoke to Galaron too, very good, the picture is becoming clearer."

"Anchorin," asked Sarah, "I also wish to ask you about some intriguing glyphs around a small pool in the garden of a house I'm buying. I wish to ask you what they mean."

Sarah rummaged around for them in her bag, and brought the notes out; she also produced a small bag, and looked at it curiously.

"Funny, I don't recall having this before," Sarah commented, "is it yours?" and she looked at Karin.

"No, I don't know anything about it," said Karin, looking puzzled, "open it up!"

Sarah opened the bag and a small quartz crystal was inside it. She instinctively gave it to Anchorin. Anchorin studied it closely, gave a slight frown and then immediately got up and placed it on a truth crystal, which safeguarded it at the same time.

"I don't like the look of it Sarah," he said, "I can activate it and see why it has been placed in your bag."

The truth crystal showered white light around the crystal, encapsulating it. From the crystal emerged an image of a priest, looking intently, and then the image faded.

"I recognised that priest! He was at Keirion's sea temple!" said Sarah, "but he was so kind and gentle, and helped us in the herb garden, that I don't feel he's involved."

"You're right! The priest has been used as a cover up for what's really going on," agreed Anchorin, "let's see if the truth crystal can dig a little deeper."

Anchorin intensified operations by asking intently for the crystal's help. The light around the crystal in question intensified, so it was almost difficult to look. Sarah, meanwhile, offered Anchorin her notes and he took them, placing them on his lap.

"Look!" exclaimed Anchorin.

Out of the dazzling light emerged an image of a figure of a man incanting. He was drawing energy out from somewhere and putting other energy back in, and then there was a collection of strange noises and the atmosphere went grey and cloudy. There was a strong sense of energy trapped in the stone, wanting to get out. The brilliant light began to fade.

"Stop!" shouted Anchorin, "switch off!" and the truth crystal de-activated, and the images and energies stopped showing.

"Someone is tampering with what we're trying to do," said Anchorin firmly, "but who?"

He opened up the notes and started examining them. A look of surprise came over his features, and he looked up.

"Sarah! These codes are part of all the glyphs Alyssia's been receiving," said Anchorin, looking intently, "do you know who owned the property before?"

"No, I tried my estate agent, and they didn't know, and the property had been with another one before a certain time. They had no idea about the pool, though of course I didn't mention any details, however, the property has been empty for up to a year," explained Sarah.

"Oh, that makes it difficult to pin any clues onto it," mused Anchorin.

"I had a dream about the pool though, but it was all positive, and it's what made me definitely want to live there," commented Sarah.

"Describe the dream exactly, there may be a clue," said Anchorin.

Sarah explained it, while Anchorin looked thoughtful, his eyes half closed as Sarah talked. When she finished, Anchorin's eyes opened and he began to speak.

"There are certain basic clues here. The pool has the typical energy of some structure used for multi-dimensional purposes, hence things appearing suddenly, scale change, and unusual perfumes, as well as voices beckoning," he explained, "that perfume, did it smell like any of these that I shall burn?"

Anchorin went to the corner of the room that had a wooden cabinet, and brought out some incense powders.

"Just let me know if any of these smell familiar," stated Anchorin.

He continued to light them one at a time, as Sarah said no to each of the first few. Then he lit one that had a combination of a very flowery fragrance with a deep musky smell.

"That's the one! I'm sure of it!" exclaimed Sarah.

Anchorin looked round with a pertinent look in his eye and spoke.

"This herb is a mind altering drug, used by those who wish to change energies and help people overcome difficult situations, but if misused in a subversive way," explained Anchorin, "it may have been used right there at your cottage to bring in the energy of the codes when Alyssia was at the fort, or accelerate the process hugely. But to what end?"

"There's a person at large who is causing problems, either from your time, Sarah, or any other time. Someone who knows the priesthood ways well and I don't like it! He has either slipped in when the vortices re-opened, or was here during the whole closure time," said Zanadar.

"He may be disguised in any kind of way," said Salaron, and he looked serious, "this activation with Alyssia may have been a reason to draw us all away from where he wishes to operate, a decoy!"

"Yes, indeed!" though we have found out a few things, despite his intentions," replied Anchorin, "perhaps to delay Maraya's rescue."

"Do you think he'd still be using my pond?" said Sarah.

"I'm not sure he'd need to return now, for he's achieved his task," replied Anchorin, "but I think you ought to return and keep a look out. I might get our Jadeir and his friends to follow on!"

"Kenny would like that," responded Karin.

"I'll come through later, see how you are when I bring Alyssia over in a day or two," said Hudlath, "but you'll let us know if anything comes up before then, won't you?"

"We certainly will, Hudlath," replied Karin, and Sarah concurred. Everyone stood up. Zanadar and Salaron said they would scout around Atlantis and communicate with the Council of Twelve from other time periods. Anchorin gave Karin, Sarah and Alyssia some of the antiviral tincture to take presently, and a supply to take back. "We'll see you soon, Alyssia," they said, giving her a hug.

"Oh no! I'd forgotten just how much day we've still got left!" exclaimed Karin, wearily clambering out of her Atlantean garments as she adjusted to twenty first century size again.

"I know! It's funny how it only hits home when we return, doesn't it!" responded Sarah.

They folded their garments and put them in the garments chest and locked it, and then went through the outer door and up via the stair well to the flat above. As they entered, the phone rang.

"Ah, you're back I hear!" cried Kenny, "any luck?" he asked, half eager and half anxious.

"We definitely know much more from our visit, and have pinpointed where she may have gone. I'll tell you the main points for now," replied Karin.

"Well, I've got the gist of it now," said Kenny, "and I'll watch out for any strange characters intent on undermining our activities."

Later Kenny returned upstairs after closing the shop, and gave Karin a big hug and then hugged Sarah too. The three of them sat down to a cup of tea.

"I had some large sales of crystals and books this afternoon, and also one of Alyssia's paintings!" commented Kenny.

"Oh good! Which one?" asked Karin.

"The one with the priest standing by a well, chanting," replied Kenny.

Karin and Sarah then told Kenny every detail about their trip.

"That's quite a lot of information to consider after a day's work!" remarked Kenny.

He sat leaning on his hand while his eyebrows drew closer together, which was his pondering position.

"When did the person come to buy Alyssia's painting?" asked Sarah.

"I think it was about 2.30pm, why do you ask?" asked Kenny.

Karin looked at Sarah slightly anxiously.

"I felt a strange chill in the air around that time and thought it was a breeze coming through an open window, until after I checked around all the rooms, they were all closed," said Sarah.

"I heard a strange whispering sound, and as I concentrated on it, it faded away, and when I began working again, it returned. After a short period it all faded away, and so did the chilly atmosphere," explained Karin.

"Right!" said Kenny, he gave a penetrating stare and frowned even more, "it sounds like this character had a definite purpose to undermine us, as I thought at the time."

"What did the person look like?" asked Sarah.

"The person concerned was male, quite tall and talkative. He said how much spiritual art was so valuable in our time to redress the balance, and the usual esoteric chatter!" here Kenny's face became serious, " I got an odd feeling about him too the longer he stayed, but I was my usual charming self. He said the image was for a friend who lived in the borders further south. I asked the powers that be, wordlessly, for Alyssia's picture to be protected, and then I got a strange feeling around me too, it was an unpleasant feeling of isolation that could have made me feel desolate if it had lasted long enough, and hadn't been to Atlantis. I seriously wondered if he knew my intentions, but something beneficent seemed to encourage me to let the transaction continue. So I let him believe I was unaware of it all, and carried on being cheerful as usual. Once he left, I asked one of the kids who had just come in, to do a bit of detective work for me and follow the guy, to see where he went. If he had a car, get the registration number, or the details if he went to a house or pub," explained Kenny.

"Did you get anything?" asked Karin.

"Yes! The lad followed him, past the central car park to just off Salop Road, and he returned with the reg number," said Kenny, producing the evidence, and placing it on the table.

"Don't you have his address details from the transaction?" asked Sarah, "so you didn't need the detective work?"

"I do have his details. I told him that I did it for each painting, but as he looked reluctant, I got him to use a bankers credit card," explained Kenny, "although that is normally enough, I wanted to get as much information as possible. I rang DVLA and made up a story to convince them to part with information, and guess what? The man seems to be a multi-property owner!"

"I hope this chap isn't just a red herring, and come to bother us in order to keep our attention going in circles," remarked Sarah.

"Well, he may be, but I think he holds a clue in all this," said Kenny, "if Jadeir was here, we'd be better off for sure. When is Hudlath coming? In a day or two?" he asked.

"Yes, perhaps it will be too late by then," said Sarah, "we should get in touch with him now."

"Where's my crystal, and I'll contact him!" exclaimed Kenny, jumping up from his chair, "I don't have enough time to be a Mr Marple anyway!" and he rushed into his bedroom.

"Hudlath! Great to see you! We've had an interesting turn of events here which needs attention, can you help?" asked Kenny.

He then explained the story to Hudlath.

"I'll send Jadeir and his friends over, and they can investigate for you!" replied Hudlath, "I'll be over later tomorrow as Alyssia's doing fine now, goodbye everyone!"

Chapter 7 – Voyage Across the Galaxy

It was around lunchtime when Hudlath and Alyssia came up the stairs to the flat door.

"Greetings!" said Hudlath; Karin greeted him cordially and hugged Alyssia.

"Sarah's gone to get some shopping and post letters. Kenny, of course, is downstairs, and Jadeir has already rushed off with his friends to check on the man who bought your painting, Alyssia," said Karin to them both, "come, sit down and I'll make some tea."

Karin soon brought the teapot and cups to the table and said she wanted to hear what had happened in Atlantis.

"Karin, you must hear about the caskets! All three of them were brought to my healing room, and I felt their energy link with the glyphs, but although it was quite dynamic and moving, it was also extremely peaceful and relaxing too. Everyone felt wonderful afterwards, full of unearthly power," Alyssia explained.

"Yes, we brought over Zanadar and Salaron, who identified the glyphs as definitely being Pleiadean. Zanadar was also able to heal Alyssia," commented Hudlath, "we knew it was important to have all three caskets together alongside the glyphs, and it was as if they catalysed each other, taking the caskets up to a higher spiritual level, as transmuters of energy and storage of greater wisdom. Perhaps the ultimate wisdom for our planet."

"Well, you can't get better than that then!" replied Karin, smiling,

"What is the next step, Hudlath?" she asked, "are we just waiting to hear from the Council of Twelve of old, as to when we have to go?"

"Yes, I've heard that Zarhavar from Cassiopeia, and Salodan from the Pleiades, have found where Maraya is, and will be in touch when they think it best for us to all go and rescue her," replied Hudlath, "you know it did puzzle me why I saw an image of Maraya looking positively radiant when she was being diverted away from the Pleiades. Well, Zarhavar intuited that the image in question we saw of her was the last impression she sent to us before being captured and drawn away. Costillo has been informed and wants to come too, as will I!"

"I'm so glad to have two men on the operation," replied Karin.

"But your help will be important too," responded Hudlath, "and it probably won't be too long before action takes place. You can be sure it will happen within a week's time, now."

"Oh! Right!" said Alyssia, trying not to look too concerned, "we'd better get some more of the other tinctures prepared, Karin, and plenty of blue mist plant too!"

Hudlath chuckled and looked at Alyssia.

"You sound a lot better! You'll be fine to go too, Alyssia," he said.

"I'd only worry about everyone if I stayed behind, anyway," replied Alyssia.

"Kenny will be upstairs in an hour's time, will you wait to see him, Hudlath?" asked Karin.

Just then a sound of footsteps and the flat door opened.

"Hello Hudlath!" cried Sarah, "here's your shopping Karin. Alyssia, how are you?" and Sarah hugged her.

"I really have to go, girls, as I sense Anchorin wishes to discuss something with me," he replied, "but I'll pop into the shop to say a quick hello," he explained, "sorry to cut it short on you Sarah, the others will no doubt explain our discussion with you."

He rose from his chair and patted Sarah's shoulder, then moved away from the table, and stood still for a moment with a look of slight concentration on his face. In an instant Hudlath's outfit had changed from Atlantean to his customary green jacket, and everyone looked astonished.

"You didn't know I could do that, did you!" and Hudlath's face broke into a grin, "it's an old Atlantean wizard trick!

"Could you teach us? Asked Sarah with a grin.

"Yes, on another occasion, and I'll let you know when we go," he replied, and then went downstairs.

Jadeir and his friends returned shortly afterwards, with the customary sound of their feet on the stairs, but they were quieter and quicker than human footfall.

"My old friends! How good to see you all," cried Jadeir, and he rushed around hugging everyone, as did the other elves, "where's the boss? Isn't he finished yet? I'll have to go and bring him upstairs, eh!!"

Jadeir gave a mischievous wink and a beaming smile. The other elves tapped on Jadeir's shoulders.

"Excuse us ever so politely, but we haven't been formally introduced to your friends yet!" they exclaimed.

Jadeir gave them a look.

"I now present to you the gracious and honourable Sarah, Alyssia and Karin," he announced in a formal voice, "and to you ladies I present these three curious elven characters, Pireus, Galen, and Calani."

However, the three elves laughed, and bowed graciously to each of the women in turn. Jadeir then wandered around to check the plants on the window sills, which were amaranth, elixir, blue mist and withering plants, and he gave out a good dose of energy to them in the form of a green tinged sparkling essence, which he sent cascading over each plant, and they visibly responded by growing a little and broadening out, as well as looking brighter.

"That will enhance your potions, my friends," said Jadeir.

"Thank you, Jadeir," responded Karin, "you just missed Hudlath, who said that the mission to find Maraya will happen within the next few days."

"Ah, I expect to stay with Kenny as I did last time, and my friends will go with you people, when the time comes," replied Jadeir.

"Well! You haven't told us what happened with that man down south, as to whether you found him?" asked Sarah.

"Oh him! Oh yes we did, and we ensured that Alyssia's painting was surrounded by such pure energy that it would make them feel uncomfortable with it, and they'd sell it on again," explained Jadeir. "We found some Atlantean herbs and replaced them with some mind altering drugs, which would make them so disorientated that they will start telling people what they've done and will probably get locked up! We also found some of the tinctures of elixir, blue mist and so on and took them away. We replaced them with a strong curry sauce!" and at this Karin burst out laughing, and the others joined in. Jadeir continued, "we also removed their crystals that were around the house. That will stop them! I'll tell Hudlath everything, so they all know in Atlantis, and whether they wish to bother taking them to the Atlantean courts," explained Jadeir, "I'll send all the items back to Anchorin's once Kenny's upstairs, so they can deal with them, in case there's any strange energies in the crystals I've not noticed, and that might also hold some clues in them too if scryed."

"Jadeir, do you think those characters have been coming through the time portals before or after the vortices were closed?" asked Sarah.

Jadeir looked thoughtful for a moment, "afterwards unfortunately. It was something I intuited from their crystals."

"I'm sure it's that vortex entanglement on the way to the Pleiades, where Maraya got diverted," replied Sarah.

"You're right there!" answered Jadeir, "I'll ask Anchorin if he's heard from the Council of Twelve whether there are any other star-way vortices in existence. I'm told there used to be many in the first days."

Two nights later, Karin and Kenny were in bed. Karin woke and looked at the clock; it was two o'clock in the morning.

"What's that light, Kenny?" asked Karin, and she sat up and peered at the wardrobe, "there's a strange sound too!"

"Eh?" muttered Kenny, and he turned over sleepily, "leave it 'til the morning, love."

Kenny's half opened eyes closed again, and he immediately drifted off again. Karin, meanwhile, gently got out of bed, trying not to disturb Kenny, went over to the wardrobe, and she opened the door. A sea of light radiated outwards.

'Oh, it's from the Atlantean wands!' thought Karin to herself, 'that's significant indeed. Perhaps I should see if Jadeir is up, he may know what it means.'

She crept out through the door to see the four elves, wide-awake and standing by the window, looking at the moon. They all turned to look at Karin when she entered the living room.

"We heard your thoughts, and it's significant, and means that we are being summoned," said Jadeir.

"Must we prepare to go now?" asked Karin, looking reluctantly.

The other elves nodded. Karin indicated that she would get dressed, while Pireus and Calani went to waken Sarah and Alyssia.

"I'll stay with Kenny, so no need to waken him again!" said Jadeir.

"We can't have any private thoughts around here, can we!" replied Karin, smiling, as she returned to the bedroom to get dressed. Jadeir's eyes twinkled mischievously.

The others stealthily crept into the living room, so as not to waken Kenny. Karin handed out some cereal bars to everyone, as well as taking some other snacks and putting them in her bag. She put more on the table for everyone to help themselves. There was quite a lot of milling around as people were picking up the food, gadgets and tinctures, and someone accidentally knocked two mugs together on the draining board when getting a cupful of water to drink, and one of them clattered into the sink. Next minute there was a groan from the bedroom and some staggering footsteps to the door. Everyone looked at each other slightly anxiously.

"Who's that?" said a sleepy Kenny, and then his eyes opened wide, "what's everyone doing up at this hour?"

"Kenny dear, we've been summoned to Atlantis," said Karin, going over to him, "we didn't want to wake you, as you've got work in the morning, though I know it seems awful to go without personally saying goodbye!"

"I see!" said Kenny, seriously, "I would have liked to have said goodbye to you, without having to find it out accidentally, though!" and he looked a little disgruntled.

"I'm sorry, dear. It was all so unexpected, and I knew you were very tired and had finally gone into a deep sleep. I didn't have the heart to wake you," Karin responded, gently.

Kenny gave her a big hug.

"Just come back in one piece!" he whispered to her.

"I will!" she whispered back.

"Has everyone got their Atlantean wands?" asked Sarah.

"Oh, I need to get mine, Kenny!" exclaimed Karin.

"Then you can all go," said Jadeir, "while I supervise the boss!" and he looked at Kenny.

"I need keeping in order!" responded Kenny, with his hands on his hips.

Alyssia and Sarah hugged Kenny, and the elves came and shook his hand animatedly. The expedition party all departed down the stairs.

"I'll set up the viewing system via your computer, to monitor their progress, like we did last time, while you get your beauty sleep," commented Jadeir.

"Yes, I need it!" replied Kenny, "thanks, mate."

He then returned to the bedroom and managed to fall asleep again quite rapidly.

Alyssia, Sarah, Karin and the elves arrived at the entrance of Anchorin's temple. For once the mountainous summit was clear of mist and everyone admired the impressive panoramic view.

"Look! I can see the sea temple and the Summer Islands!" cried Karin.

103

"I've spotted the Garden of Eden!" said Alyssia, "it's fantastic. I hope we could all visit it one day."

Alyssia found it difficult to turn away from the view of the Garden of Eden, and her mind kept on pondering on it for some time. Once inside the temple, her thoughts turned elsewhere temporarily.

"Come in, come in!" ushered Anchorin as everyone had entered through the temple doors and were walking down the corridor to the customary meeting room. Inside stood three members of the Council of Twelve, Zanadar, Aurion and Salaron.

"Greetings all!" said Zanadar, and everyone else exchanged their greetings too.

"To business!" announced Anchorin, "Costillo will be arriving shortly and so will Hudlath. Apologies for being called in the small hours, but you can catch up on sleep once on the spaceship. Zanadar, do you know when Zarhavar and the others will be arriving?"

"It won't be long now, Anchorin," replied Zanadar, and he inclined his head a little as if to sense their movements, "I believe they've been to a distant planet, and should be here within half an hour."

"There will be time for you all to have some refreshments before you go, then!" said Anchorin.

He turned his head towards the door with a look of concentration. Within moments there was a knock at the door, and on opening it under Anchorin's instruction, two priests entered, carrying some food and drink on trays for them all. Everyone except the Council of Twelve members got up to sample the food.

"The food's excellent!" said Alyssia, "don't you eat much?" she asked Zanadar.

Zanadar smiled, "we don't need to consume much, only drinking water while we are in the three dimensional worlds. Once out of that, we just ask for energy from the Source."

"That's very handy! I wish I could do without it, as food is so expensive in our time period," responded Alyssia.

Costillo and Hudlath entered, and they were greeted by everyone, and also sat down to eat and drink. Anchorin quietly called one of his priests to inform him when the Council of Twelve members would arrive.

Everyone was aware of a subtle vibration emanating from somewhere above the temple, and looked instinctively upwards, and at each other.

"It's got to be Zarhavar and friends!" cried Hudlath.

Not much longer after that, a priest knocked on the door, and Anchorin affirmed for the door to be opened. In stepped a taller orange-pink faced being similar to Zanadar who bowed courteously to everyone.

"Greetings! We are here and ready to transport our friends now!" he exclaimed.

"Good!" announced Anchorin, "well, everyone! From all of us here in the temple, we wish you good fortune, and will send our prayers and strong healing energy via our crystals!" and he ushered everyone outside the temple.

"We shall keep in close contact as much as we can, Anchorin, and Zanadar!" said Zarhavar.

Zarhavar looked at Anchorin and the three Council of Twelve members, Zanadar, Aurion and Salaron, and then up into the heavens. Alyssia and the others also looked up to see Zanadar's spaceship with the older time period spaceship hovering alongside.

"Come over and stand underneath our ship," said Zarhavar, "and we'll all ascend into the ship once the main beam is activated."

Zanadar, Aurion and Salaron stood outside the circle of people waiting to board ship, and Anchorin joined the three of them. A white beam of energy shone down upon the group, then a pulsating energy came briefly. Anchorin, Zanadar and the others gave the greeting sign, and the group about to ascend reciprocated with the same response. Everyone began to rise gently upwards to the ship's entrance on the underside. Once inside the ship, they found themselves hovering over towards the floor beside the entrance, and then the doorway closed. Anchorin and the Council members went indoors a moment to discuss monitoring what they could of this expedition. Zarhavar and their Council of Twelve spaceship disappeared into the earlier time period 11,000 years previous, to begin their journey towards the Pleiades that would link to the route nearby that led to Pelucia.

"Kenny! I'm through to the Council of Twelve spaceship!" exclaimed Jadeir.

"Can you see the group yet?" asked Kenny sleepily, as he'd been dozing on the sofa.

"Ah! There's Karin and Alyssia. I'll see if we can contact them directly," replied Jadeir.

He zoomed in on them. Unlike the last trip into space, the group were travelling in comfort, and had their own rooms. Kenny came over and sat by Jadeir.

"Well? Have you made contact then?" he asked eagerly.

"Sorry, I think they're asleep after all," replied Jadeir, resignedly.

Kenny groaned.

"Well, try another room, perhaps Costillo and Hudlath are nearby," urged Kenny.

Jadeir searched around several rooms. Many of them were empty, except one where there were two beds with people lying in them. Jadeir focused in closer on seeing a grey beard on one person and dark hair on the other. All of a sudden, the grey bearded man sat up and looked around with alert eyes. His face was thin and he had a sleeved tunic on which came down to his knees. He leapt out of bed and began a series of vigorous yogic and athletic exercises.

"Well, that doesn't look like Hudlath, does it?" said Jadeir with a grin.

Kenny laughed, "not really!"

The man's eyes narrowed slightly.

"Who's there? There's someone watching me, I can tell!" he shouted.

The person in the other bed stirred a little for a moment.

"Time to go!" stated Jadeir, and he swiftly tried the next room, "ah! There they are, at last!"

"They're asleep too!" said Kenny.

"Well, at least we know they're safe and well at present, anyway," responded Jadeir.

"May as well get some more kip then!" yawned Kenny, and he wandered back to the sofa and fell asleep instantly.

Jadeir continued to examine the spaceship's interior for a while longer. Finally he discovered where the Council of Twelve's headquarters was situated.

"Greetings Zarhavar, I am Jadeir the elf, from Anchorin's time. I am with Kenny in Oswestry, and just letting you know I'm making contact, and I saw that the travellers are fine!" he explained.

"Good! Did you have a good look around then?" questioned Zarhavar, with a hint of humour.

"Well, yes I did, but not prying of course," explained Jadeir, with a slightly coy look.

"Oh, of course not!" replied Zarhavar.

"However, I did see a strange man, who I initially thought was Hudlath until he leapt out of bed like a winged horse, and began to do vigorous exercises. He then started exclaiming that he was being watched, and asked who it was. I moved away quickly after that!" remarked Jadeir, "who was he?"

"Oh, that was only Jaysangar," replied Zarhavar, "he's harmless enough really. We're taking him to one of the planets in the Pylon of Phairos star group, as he needs to learn new ways of living. I'm sure it will do him good!"

"Yes, I'm sure. The Pylon of Phairos is linked to the sixth and seventh dimensions, isn't it?" asked Jadeir.

"Indeed! Though they can operate on third and fourth too. The inhabitants can live inside light structures quite happily, and concentrate on energy creation, and building the subtle energies surrounding star systems and life forms, and is a place that teaches many devas who operate on lots of planets. Jaysangar has tremendous energy for his age, and wishes to put it to good use," explained Zarhavar, "maybe he will even progress to create light structures himself!"

"Fascinating! It has been interesting talking to you, Zarhavar. Please give my regards to our group. I must go now and rest, even us elves need an hour or two occasionally!" replied Jadeir.

"Yes my friend, I shall. Goodbye now," said Zarhavar, and waved.

Jadeir focused the crystal to just linking with the door to Karin and Alyssia's room, and then he stirred Kenny.

"Boyo! I need some beauty sleep!" he cried.

"Ahh, you're beautiful enough," muttered Kenny, sleepily, with eyes still closed, "I need to keep practicing."

However, after a few minutes Kenny stirred, and he went to take sentry duty at the crystal operated monitor, while Jadeir rested.

All was very quiet on board the spaceship for just over half an hour, and Kenny found himself half dozing because of it. Then he heard a bedroom door opening gently, so he focused the crystal to see where the sound was coming from, and looked down a corridor route which was L shaped.

'Ah, this is where we began the search for the group. It's that character, Jaysangar and his mate!' thought Kenny very quietly, 'the dark haired one looks a bit like a younger Jaysangar. Must be a grandson!'

The pair wandered along to the control room, and Kenny followed their movements. Naturally, not wishing to draw attention to himself, Kenny kept at a distance from them.

"Good, you're here!" said Zarhavar, "you may as well sit down here until we reach the disembarking zone."

Kenny noticed the panoramic front window area of the spaceship, and through it he could see some spangling looking planets not too far away.

'It's the Pylon of Phairos group! They're beautiful!' he thought.

Jaysangar looked alert again and stood up. Kenny realised in his enthusiasm, his thoughts had been too loud on seeing the beauty of the planets ahead.

"I'm being watched again, I know it! Zarhavar, there's an odd presence on board! It has to be dealt with," he demanded.

For some reason Jaysangar wasn't able to view people via the crystals, and in any case he wasn't clairsentient enough to be a priest.

"Calm down, Jaysangar!" replied Zarhavar firmly, "the presence you sense is only a man called Kenny, who is wanting to talk to the group who are presently asleep. One of the ladies is his wife, and they are going on a mission to rescue a friend from a distant planet."

Zarhavar smiled in the direction where Kenny was viewing from, and Kenny waved in response. Jaysangar looked chastened.

"I'm so sorry, I couldn't see who it was, and I've come from a time period where you have to be alert and deal with trouble constantly," he explained, "so it's my first instinct to respond the way I do."

He looked up at Zarhavar and put his hand in his pocket, searched through the contents, and brought his hand out again. He stood up and went over to Zarhavar, opened his palm, and offered what was on it to him.

"I wish to give the wife this little charm. It is an amulet to give strength and determination, as well as alertness to whoever wears it. I owe it to the man!" explained Jaysangar, kindly.

"Thank you, Jaysangar," replied Zarhavar, and he smiled and turned to the crystal, "can you hear this, Kenny?"

"Yes I can. Please thank Jaysangar for me," responded Kenny.

"He heard, and thanks you," said Zarhavar, and Jaysangar smiled happily.

The planet of choice, like some of its neighbours, was surrounded by a beautiful opalescent atmosphere, which emanated a strong feeling of peace to all who came to it. The ship descended through the levels of the atmosphere, from gold and rainbow sparkles to streaks of iridescent layers of light energy instead of clouds, to a layer of air that was a pale violet several thousand feet above ground, down through the spectrum to a pale red at ground level. The gold sparkles above the violet were of differing shades and metallic, and on many occasions could be dazzling, and when that happened it rained down in light showers of those golden sparkles through the atmosphere.

The ship hovered within the golden areas, and then gently descended a little until it was within the violet layer. The entrance hatch opened, and the beam was activated. Jaysangar and his sibling were standing near the entrance by now. They waved to Zarhavar and the other members of the Council of Twelve who were there now. Then they were lifted up from the floor and then gently transported through the hatch door and down to the ground.

Once landed, Zarhavar closed the hatch, returned to the helm and ascended again to continue on the star-way towards the Pleiades. He turned to look at Kenny.

"Still there?" and smiled, "the next constellation is Orion, and we will be passing Rigel's planets directly. They are just as spectacular as the Pylon of Phairos."

"It's a pity everyone's missing all this beauty," remarked Kenny.

"There's still plenty of it for a while yet!" replied Zarhavar.

Salodan and Aurial had come through a moment ago, and did some work with the controls a moment and then turned to greet Kenny.

They then assumed their places back at the controls, near to where Zarhavar was standing. The three of them looked intently at each other and then resumed concentration on the job of transporting the ship. Kenny could see pinpoints of light outside, sometimes silver, sometimes gold, and also iridescent streaks, sometimes fleeting and other times present for several minutes. Aurial, from Sirius, gave indication to the others, looked at Kenny and smiled.

"I see our visitor is still watching!" he remarked, "hello Kenny!" and Kenny greeted him, "did you know that our native friends from the Pleiades will meet us at the junction

109

with the Pelucian star-way, and may accompany us for a while."

"That's very reassuring, Aurial," replied Kenny, "how long will it take to get to both Rigel and that junction?" he asked.

"Rigel usually takes about three hours, and it should take about three to fours hours to reach the junction from there, and six or seven hours in total" replied Aurial.

"I hope it won't be too long before the group wakes up as I feel I'll need to sleep again shortly," commented Kenny, "you will get Jadeir to wake me if they become active when I'm asleep! He's liable to get chatting to his elf friends and forget!"

Zarhavar smiled, "don't worry, I'll remember!"

"I'll just remind him to wake up too!" replied Kenny.

He stepped away from the screen temporarily to shake Jadeir.

"Hey boyo! I need my beauty sleep now!" cried Kenny.

"You're beautiful enough. I need to keep practicing," responded Jadeir, with closed eyes.

After a few minutes, Jadeir opened his eyes wide; looked around with an alert stare, and sent bright cascades of energy to all the plants in the flat. He then leapt up, giving Kenny a broad grin.

"Ok, your turn on the sofa, now!" he said.

"Thanks Jadeir, but don't forget to tell me when everyone's awake. I told Zarhavar to remind you!" insisted Kenny.

"Message understood, my friend!" responded Jadeir, "goodnight!"

Kenny lay down, and slight sounds of snoring were soon apparent after a few minutes. Jadeir waved to Zarhavar and began chatting to him, then his elf friends appeared and they talked for a while.

Images of codes appeared before Kenny's eyes, the one's Sarah had shown him, as found at Ty Bach Craig; but in this instance he was whirring through space, and the codes were approaching him relentlessly, and repeated continuously. He reckoned their source was the Pleiades, but they also resonated from the Pylon of Phairos, Rigel, and all their planets, since they were all on the same frequency. Why was he seeing them here, and were they some of the codes that Alyssia had received?

Kenny awoke to the sound of Jadeir singing to the plants, and he just happened to sing one note rather louder than the others in close proximity to Kenny's ear.

"Good morning, Kenny boyo!" sang Jadeir chirpily, on seeing Kenny stir, "as I'm helping the plants to rise upwards, I thought I'd do the same for you!"

"You're such a kind fellow!" mumbled Kenny, with half-opened eyes, "what time is it?"

"Six thirty exactly!" chimed Jadeir.

Kenny frowned, "What!!" he exclaimed.

"Karin wants to speak to you!" replied Jadeir.

Kenny's sleepy eyes opened wide, and he jumped up, rushing past Jadeir to the computer screen.

He saw Karin's face there and began talking to her.

"Karin! How are you, and what's happening next?" he asked.

"I'm fine, and so is everyone else. It's a very peaceful experience on board the Council of Twelve spaceship. It feels so safe and comfortable," replied Karin.

"Have you reached Rigel yet?" asked Kenny.

"Yes, we've just passed Rigel, and due to come to that change over of star-ways within the next hour; but because of the strange energies created by the intermingling of those star-ways, the Council of Twelve are going to lift out of the star-way and travel towards the Pelucian one cutting off a corner. They said we might feel a bit of motion, like being in an aeroplane when experiencing air pockets, but not to worry about anything as we shall remain safe whilst in the spaceship," she explained.

"What will the other star-way be like to travel along?" asked Kenny.

"It won't have any harmonious planets and star systems around like the Pylon of Phairos or Rigel once we get past the outer planets of the Hyadean ring. Also, there may be some discomfort, as it is not as harmonious and filled with light as the Pleiadean star-way. The ship will have more difficulty in regulating speeds due to the degree of gravitational pull from the fourth dimensional planets and suns, which would have been protected in a fifth dimensional star-way. Though the fact that it is a star-way, means it is still perfectly possible for spaceships to travel along it without being endangered," explained Karin.

"Yes, I see, dear. I just hope you don't get the equivalent of jet-lag on board," replied Kenny.

"Don't worry. I'll keep you informed as often as I can," said Karin, "but there may be occasions when it might not be possible, like when we hit some turbulence, or possibly after the Hyadean group."

"Karin, Zarhavar told me that the Pleiadeans would escort you all for a while, have they appeared yet?" asked Kenny.

"Not yet dear, but Zarhavar did mention that they would be here just before we exit the star-way to get past that spaghetti junction spot!" responded Karin.

"Ok, go carefully, dear. I'm sure you're in the safest hands around!" replied Kenny.

Karin smiled and blew Kenny a kiss, and he returned one too.

Galen and the two other elves then crowded around the screen as Karin departed, and called out for Jadeir. They all began talking together while Kenny returned to the sofa and fell asleep again for another hour.

Kenny and Jadeir were sitting at the table having an early breakfast, when Kenny started to tell Jadeir about his dream. The computer screen had been angled so that they could still view it while eating. They could see everyone on board strapping themselves into seats, including Zarhavar, while that interim period of flying from one star-way to another took place.

"Right everyone! Time for some antics!" exclaimed Zarhavar, "our Pleiadean friends are arriving and are drawing near at this moment to support our energy systems. Take some amaranth if you feel you need to, and that will help any discomfort while travelling."

The Oswestry group and Costillo took the Atlantean herb provided by the Council of Twelve, which they had put into their waist pouches previously.

Alyssia and Karin were sitting with everyone else, strapped into their seats. They looked out through the anterior screen as the spaceship wheeled around the knotted star-way junction, and could see the Pleiadean spaceship coming in closer to accompany them.

"I can feel a beam of energy surrounding me, and it's coming from that craft, can you?" asked Alyssia.

"Yes I can!" replied Karin, "and I think it's stabilising everyone, including our spaceship."

The craft lurched upwards diagonally, away from the star-way and wheeled around a little as it circumnavigated the knotted junction of the star-ways, and glided downwards to the Pelucian star-way.

"Now about to enter the Pelucian star-way everyone!" announced Zarhavar.

There was a sudden jolt and juddering motion for a moment, which vibrated through the whole craft, and then they were inside the star-way. The Pleiadean craft still flew beside them, but it remained outside the star-way.

"I'll warn you of moments when we may have to get seated again. I can't guarantee to know every moment, as this star-way has been tampered with, of course," advised Zarhavar.

Everyone then undid their seatbelts and got up. Salodan who was from the Pleiades, Costillo, Sarah, Karin and Alyssia all approached Karin's crystal, which had been safely clamped onto a small pedestal fitting on the spaceship's control panels, in an area set aside for communication crystals. They gave their greetings to Kenny and Jadeir, just before Kenny went to open the shop. Hudlath came over as well, having had a quick word with Zarhavar. Salodan adjusted a control nearby to the crystal.

"The codes as described to me as seen in your dreams, Kenny, are what are used to maintain the star-ways, Kenny," explained Salodan, the Pleiadean member of the Council of Twelve, "it is interesting that you had that dream, for we are utilising the potency of those codes as we progress, in order to re-establish the good energy of this star-way before it was diverted to Pelucia."

"How do you use these codes?" questioned Kenny.

"We project them along the star-way via the spaceship's energetic resources, as you saw in your dream, and see them permanently linked to that star-way, emanating good energy constantly," explained Salodan, "they do have other uses, but that will be perceived in time by the group. We will teach them about the codes as we travel."

"I see, the codes have many purposes! I look forward to hearing more about them as you all progress," replied Kenny, "by the way, do we need to link in all the time?"

"Not necessary. Maybe two or three times today, for now, and we'll see how far we've got by then, my friends," responded Salodan, "I must return to my duties now."

"Understood!" said Kenny, "goodbye Salodan."

Salodan smiled to him and departed off to another part of the ship. "I shall have to go and open the shop now, and hope to speak to you later. Goodbye Karin, goodbye everyone!"

They all responded in turn as Kenny departed.

Jadeir waved to the others, and they departed too, allowing Jadeir and his elf friends to talk together for a period of time, before allowing the crystal to go into resting mode until lunchtime when Kenny would return.

An hour or two later, Jadeir became invisible and walked quietly downstairs to the door into the shop. He opened the door a crack to see if anyone was present; luckily there was no one in the annexe, except for a customer near the annexe looking at one of Alyssia's paintings on the far wall, so his back was turned. Jadeir slipped through the door and approached Kenny, becoming visible for a moment when no one was looking.

"Yoo hoo! I'm off to Pistyl Rhaeadr as Zarhavar said we don't need to look at the screen all the time now. It's in resting mode until you go upstairs, boyo!" he said.

"Since when did anyone give you permission to sneak off when I'm working hard?" replied Kenny, telepathically.

"Zarhavar's orders!" replied Jadeir, "I won't be longer than an hour, my friend!"

Kenny pulled a slightly wry expression and smiled.

"I don't know! Off you go then!" he replied.

Jadeir laughed and began his departure, saying, "I'll definitely be back by lunchtime!"

Chapter 8 – Healing the Pelucian Star-way

As the spaceship was beginning along the Pelucian star-way, one of the Pleiadean crew projected his spirit body to visit everyone in the spaceship.

"Hello all, my name is Selahon. I've projected my spirit because to cross the wall of a star-way even in our Pleiadean bodies would not be comfortable. We are projecting energy to you all to help you adjust to this star-way. Apparently this star-way's final destination was originally not Pelucia, but at the far end of the huge constell-ation of Eridanus, the very large star of Achernar. Pelucia is over towards Reticulum. The energy is rather chaotic at times along this star-way as far as we can see, because the energy is being drained off by whoever manipulated this star-way originally."

"Can I ask if there are other star-ways in our universe which have been tampered with?" asked Karin.

"Luckily, none! It is because the Eridanus route is so long, and for various reasons, many of us travellers have not been along it for a while, and only noticed something was suspicious when the two star-ways became locked together," answered Selahon.

"Will you be travelling with us for very far?" asked Hudlath, "and will there be hazards we must anticipate along the way?"

"We will travel part of the way, but your Council of Twelve member from Andromeda, Sirdal, has contacted home planet to request another escorting spaceship to continue from where we will leave you," replied Selahon, "at the outer reaches beyond the Hyadean planetary ring. They will travel with you for a good length of the journey and will assist if any problems occur."

"Is travelling outside the star-way better or worse at present?" queried Hudlath.

"It is stable enough for us, and will be for our journey. It is later on when it could get quite difficult, we aren't sure what to expect, and it may not be such an advantage to remain inside the star-way, the only advantage is that it's the route to follow for your destination," answered Selahon, "well, I must return to my duties now, and hope we may meet again under better circumstances!"

Everyone said farewell to Selahon, and he departed.

"If you all want to go and relax for a while, and then Salodan would be happy to give you an introductory talk about the codes. So, if sleep beckons you, get it now while you can!" announced Zarhavar.

A crew member appeared, and escorted the group along the corridors to their rooms.

"Here is your room, ladies," he said, looking at Alyssia, Sarah and Karin and giving them a friendly smile.

They went inside, looked around briefly, and then turned, giving an inquiring look to see where the others would be staying.

"Everyone else will be in adjacent rooms, so they'll be easy enough to find!" replied the crew member.

They watched Costillo and Hudlath being shown to the next room, and the three elves, Galen, Pireus and Calani enter the third one in line.

"Where are the beds?" asked Sarah.

"You must have to press a button somewhere, and they'll pop up!" answered Karin, "have a look!"

There were cries of laughter from the next room.

"I think they've found theirs!" responded Alyssia, "why don't we ask them how they did it?"

"Good idea!" chorused Sarah and Karin.

They peeked their heads in on Costillo and Hudlath.

"We heard the laughter and thought you must have found the beds!" said Sarah.

"We did!" replied Hudlath, still chuckling, "but Costillo pressed a button which he thought brought down his bed, but it turned out to be an overall command switch to fold them both away! And guess who felt as if he was being pushed off a hoverbuggy in a hurry!"

"We'll give you a demonstration!" announced Costillo, "gather round ladies!"

He pointed to a cream coloured button at shoulder level beside him.

"I'll press this now!" and there was a small sound like a piano key being sounded, followed by a door sliding. Everyone was looking all around but couldn't see where it was coming from until the expected beds descended from the ceiling. The mattresses were aligned vertically initially, and then they rotated to horizontal as they touched the floor.

"My! Four posters, that's posh!" exclaimed Sarah.

Costillo pulled back the cover of the one nearest to him, to reveal the pillow and night attire.

"I can't believe it, and there's night clothes under the cover too, isn't that lovely and thoughtful," remarked Alyssia.

"They certainly think of everything here. The dangerous button you need to avoid until you are finished with the beds completely is this yellow one just above the cream one!" explained Costillo.

"Thanks Costillo, and sweet dreams," said Karin.

"Enjoy your rest horizontally!" said Alyssia.

"Bon voyage!" said Sarah.

"No more voyages on this bed, thanks!" cried Hudlath, as the others departed with a responding chuckle.

Everyone had a good rest for just over and hour, and were awakened by a gently melody through a tannoy in their rooms.

"Greetings, my friends! This is Zarhavar speaking. Please make your way to the bridge where you can have something to eat and then meet Salodan for the introductory talk about the codes. Thank you."

"That was a really good rest. I feel wide awake and alert, and we've only been asleep for just over and hour," exclaimed Alyssia.

"They must have put crystals in the mattresses!" responded Sarah, and they laughed.

Karin bent down and examined the mattress closely.

"Hey, you could be right, the mattress is covered in tiny iridescent jewels," cried Karin.

"Really?" asked Sarah.

Sarah and Alyssia came over to look.

Hudlath, Costillo, Alyssia, Karin, Sarah and the three elves, Galen, Pireus and Calani were at the bridge a few minutes later, and were offered a snack. Zarhavar was there, overseeing navigation control.

"I trust you all slept well?" he smiled cheerfully, "I know you have discovered why; the secret is in the iridescent crystals on your mattresses brought from the Pylon of Phairos!"

"Very impressive, my friend!" responded Hudlath.

About twenty minutes later Salodan hurried in, and stopped in front of the group. They had just finished their snacks a few minutes ago.

"Sorry to keep you all waiting. Right! If you'd like to come to my conference room, we can discuss the codes more effectively there," he said, and ushered everyone out through another door, "it's straight to that open door with the pink light inside the room. I just need to have a moment's talk with Zarhavar, and I'll be back!"

Everyone walked through, while Salodan approached Zarhavar. They looked at each other, and then at the view of space outside, and they wordlessly exchanged a thought of concern about the route they were taking, and a growing sense of urgency required.

"An hour, that is all we have, in reality!" whispered Zarhavar, and Salodan nodded.

"We could still do it!" Salodan replied; then he turned and followed the others to the pink-lit room.

Salodan knew that the Pleiadeans were busy at present, and would be unable to stay much longer, and the next ship would be arriving sometime soon. They had to begin code projecting themselves in earnest before the hour expired.

"Everyone! The object of this exercise is that we need to get you all familiar with the codes, as they will be very essential in order to heal and lift the energy of this star-way. The codes are divided into ten groups, and within each group they are subdivided into two lots of seven sets. They are based on the main chakras of the body, and two per set, left-brained and right-brained, so there are fourteen in each group," explained Salodan.

He walked up to a screen and pressed a control button nearby, and two images of eyes with surrounding symbolic imagery appeared.

"Here are the first two images. This group is called "Awakening to spirituality," he instructed.

Two images like radiant eyes appeared. The right-brained one had four blue spheres in the centre of the eye's iris, which was bright yellow, and the eye was surrounded in the same colour. On the right was a mauve Maltese cross, and on the left, a magenta heart. For the left-brained image, the iris had a white diamond tinged around the edge with yellow and an orange border. From each side a shaft of yellow light with orange borders emanated. On the right was a white diamond like the centre of the eye, and on the left a diamond within which was imaged the diamond and four shafts of light like in the centre.

"The right-brained image brings through this energy from higher sources, and the left-brained ones help to integrate into the bodily system. The four spheres of blue are the four elements, with the fifth element as the pupil underneath. The diamonds in the left-brained image denote alertness and bringing in energy from the right-brained image, and transmitting that to the body to integrate this," explained Salodan. "We can use these images to heal ourselves, but in this instance, to project energy outwards along the star-way. If you could study the notes here, but just take a few minutes. You don't need to know everything; just get acquainted enough with the images to be able to understand the principles of it all. We need your help in projecting them, as more powerful intent is required as soon as possible, and the crew are already busy."

"This sounds rather urgent, is that right?" asked Hudlath, with a curious expression in his eyes.

"We realised that we would need more help in this task, and so we appeal for your help. Will you join us?" asked Salodan, hopefully.

"Yes, of course," replied Hudlath, "are we not agreed everyone?"

The group cried a resounding yes. Salodan almost had to hold his hands over his ears.

"Will we be using the other sets as well?" asked Alyssia, "and how long will it take for a set to work?"

"Good question!" replied Salodan, "we can't say for sure, but we will know more clearly when all of you begin with the first step. Please follow me to the energy projection room."

They all followed Salodan back along the corridor towards the bridge, and just before the bridge's entrance, they went through a door to their left. It was a beautifully quiet room, with a glow of violet light spangled with gold and magenta. Crystalline pieces of an iridescent hue lined the walls, and a circle of stands were arranged in the centre of the room.

"It's like Anchorin's crystal healing room!" exclaimed Alyssia.

"Correction! Anchorin's healing room is based on our design!" replied Salodan, and as he smiled, small illuminated stars gently emanated from his eyes, and seemed to hover overhead, making the room feel positively still and deeply peaceful.

"We placed these crystals in an arc formation, which would be pointing towards this star-way ahead, in particular," continued Salodan, "for us to project energy effectively."

He reached for some impressive sized quartz crystals that had a rainbow-tinged sheen, and placed one on each of the stands, and strapped them on safely with the attachments found on the stands. They consisted of two small straight crystals attached alongside one bigger, central one; so all the crystals were parallel.

"They are a kind of cluster, aren't they?" asked Sarah, "most beautiful."

Everyone was examining them carefully.

"Pylon of Phairos?" asked Hudlath.

"Yes indeed, they specialise in amazing crystals," replied Salodan, "now, could you go to that drawer over there," he asked, pointing to a lilac set of small drawers flush with the wall nearby, "the top one, and take out the first card set for each of you, thank you!"

Karin reached for the cards and brought them over. Salodan placed one left-brained, and one right-brained chakra image into a retractable tray, like in a DVD player. He then pressed a button and the images appeared illuminated under the crystals. He did this with all seven crystal clusters, so that the whole card set was out.

"I just want you all to keep an eye on these crystals, to ensure that they are still pointing the right way and that the image projection is as strong as possible. Also, the ideal is that you must work through all the cards yourselves individually before working on the star-way; it should only take a few minutes for you to gain insight, with the powerful crystals on board. Once achieved, then could each of you take a couple of the cards per chakra and focus on them simultaneously, while the eighth person looks after the crystals by enhancing your energy to them with the eighth crystal there and monitors progress. You can rotate your duties every so often, but the first hour is critical for seeing results. I must leave you now to return to other duties, but you can contact Zarhavar by intercom for any advice. There are more set ones in that drawer."

Everyone set to work as Salodan left the room. The three elves had done their processing in a flash and were projecting their energy already, and sat cross-legged facing the crystals. The others in the group caught up and conferred on who would do which couple of cards remaining after the elves chose theirs. The group settled down to their projection work. The room was silent and filled with the strong energy of the code projection. They had their eyes shut while doing this, so only the overseer at the crystals could see what was happening out in the star-way.

Hudlath was the overseer at present, and he aided the crystals in their projection. He could see a lot of the energy reaching outwards, entering the star-way, and could sense it

120

was beginning to brighten up in the area ahead that was visible, and was helping to maintain the sea-green colour.

Alyssia saw something flashing out of the corner of her eye, even with her eyes closed, and then the tannoy became active.

"We are reaching the outer circuits of the Hyadean satellite planets," announced Zarhavar, "we are expecting the ship from Andromeda at any moment! Then the Pleiadean ship will leave. You are all doing well with your projection."

"We appear to be maintaining the correct energy level at present, Zarhavar," answered Hudlath, "for now."

"Yes, I am endeavouring to estimate how far your energising reaches along the star-way, and will know more once my crystal bank estimator comes up with some information," replied Zarhavar.

A moving white dot became visible ahead of them, and soon spotted by them all.

"I hope it's from Andromeda!" cried Sarah, peering ahead.

"It is!" responded Hudlath, "I received an acknowledgement symbol from them.

The tannoy became active again.

"Good news as you'll know by now," said Zarhavar, "the Andromeda ship is approaching fast. You can all relax a moment once I give you the message that their craft will take over the projecting, until you have worked with the second set of cards, and begin to project them."

The spaceship was now approaching very close to the Council of Twelve's ship. The ship shone bright silver, with a pale mauve glow around it, and a pinky-gold sparkling light revolved around the central hub of the ship.

"All right everyone! You can leave the crystals for now. Please focus on the second set now," announced Zarhavar.

Everyone duly went to the purple drawer and extracted a set each of the second group, and began to work on them.

Zarhavar gazed out of the viewing screen to see the space ship hovering nearby. He could see the energy being projected down the star-way. A figure was also projecting himself across to the Council of Twelve's spaceship, and appeared near Zarhavar.

"Greetings, Zarhavar, I am Sirankal. As you can see we are projecting energy now. We have a good sized crew with us, so we can keep this going as long as necessary."

"Thank you, Sirankal," replied Zarhavar, "I am preparing an estimation of how far along the star-way the energy is flowing, and what state it is in at present."

"Good, that will be useful, the better it is, the faster our ships will be able to go, of course," replied Sirankal, "your friend needs to be rescued urgently!"

"It's going to take several days to reach the planet at this speed, unlike the other star-ways. Hindered intentionally," uttered Zarhavar, with a pensive look.

"What sized crystals do you have in your projection room?" asked Sirankal.

"They range from about one foot to one and a half feet, why?" asked Zarhavar.

"I was just thinking that either more crystals or our bigger ones would help speed up the process," explained Sirankal, "we have some three to four foot long ones from our favourite supplier planet obtained recently, the Pylon of Phairos. The ones we are using are that size, but we have some surplus ones," explained Sirankal.

"Let's see them!" exclaimed Zarhavar eagerly, "were they from the golden Mount?"

"Yes, they found much bigger crystals more recently there. I'll get the crew to pack them on our little transporter craft and bring them over," replied Sirankal.

"Thank you Sirankal, that would be excellent. Three to four feet, marvellous! We'll be speeding along with that size!" replied Zarhavar eagerly.

"I'll return to my craft and get the cargo moving, my friend," replied Sirankal.

He smiled and then disappeared back to his ship. About ten minutes later, Zarhavar saw a small craft exiting a docking station on the near flank of the Andromedan ship. It fared well in the atmosphere because the Andromedan craft was inside the star-way, with the anticipated intent of supplying the crystals and ensuring that they would be delivered safely, without the transporter craft having to negotiate the star-way barrier. The craft docked into the Council of Twelve's space ship, and Zarhavar saw the crew members enter the ship, bringing the heavy load of crystals one by one up to the projection room.

"If you would just follow my crew members, they will show you where in the projection room they can be placed," said Zarhavar.

He asked four of his crew members to help the Andromedans. They knocked on the projection room door, and Hudlath opened it.

"Excuse me, we are bringing larger crystals from the Andromedan ship to use for projection," explained one of the crew, "we've come to put them on the stands."

"Please enter!" responded Hudlath, "is it alright to stop projecting?"

"Yes, the Andromedan ship is doing that to cover us all very satisfactorily at present," replied the crew member.

"Ok everyone! Just stop projecting now, we have a new batch of crystal replacements arriving now!" announced Hudlath.

Everyone opened their eyes and blinked a little, then moved away from the crystals on their stands. The crew soon had the smaller crystals removed and put away, then slotted in some supports onto the stands to hold the larger crystals, which were carefully lowered onto the padded supports and strapped in along their sides, ensuring that they were angled correctly towards the star-way's route.

"You'll definitely see an improvement," said one of the Andromedan crew.

"Good! Excellent!" replied Hudlath, "let's get back to work everyone!"

"Yes boss!" replied the elves, and Hudlath gave them a wry look as they chuckled.

The larger crystals improved the codes' work, and as the first set of codes had sent the energies of the eye images along the star-way, now, with the second set, diamonds being the predominant symbol, so those images were being projected. The result of that being that the star-way route was maintaining its colour of pale turquoise.

"The first card set opens the way," mused Alyssia.

"And the second set begins to bring in energy," responded Sarah.

"Are we moving faster, Hudlath?" asked Karin.

"Yes we are, we're going nearly twice as fast according to a dial I've just noticed," replied Hudlath, "though it slows a little if we don't concentrate fully."

Everyone continued to concentrate hard on focusing on the cards and crystals simultaneously. About an hour later, the tannoy sang out and Zarhavar spoke.

"Greetings all! You are welcome to stop concentrating now, for your larger crystals have more reserve capacity than the others to drive the ship at the same pace for a while. They will only need a top up input every three hours now. However, I wish for you to concentrate on the third set and get them projected for half an hour's stint, and then leave it for three hours. But, come my friends, before you do that, get some refreshments in the main room," explained Zarhavar.

They all made their way through, gathering near Zarhavar while eating and drinking.

"We will stop for a good feast later, after you have done the third set of cards, as each set helps to raise the speed of the ship. I know you are tired, so will ask you to do the fourth and fifth sets tomorrow, and then our speed will be good by then," commented Zarhavar, "we may even reach our destination in another day or two from now, which is promising," and his eyes glowed, "I don't think our Pelucian friends will be expecting us to arrive so soon!"

"How will we surprise them when our way is lit up ahead of us?" asked Hudlath.

"Well, we might have to endure the darker energy to a degree when we approach, but we have another possible trick!" and Zarhavar smiled slightly, "we will still light the way ahead, but cloak it in a dark coloured shield as we go, so nothing can be seen from afar!"

"What does your cloak consist of?" asked Hudlath.

"It is particles of matter, or rather, antimatter, which is held suspended in formation through use of a force field of electro-magnetic energy around that. The particles of anti-matter appear dark because they obscure light," explained Zarhavar, "and is a substance we use to propel the craft."

"I see," said Hudlath, with interest, "we've had no need for secrecy in my age, and hope it isn't discovered until towards the end of Atlantis, but having been there, I rather think it would be used then, we just didn't detect it at the time."

"That is the situation usually, you don't notice it, and the objects aren't detectable on most equipment, and would only appear as a black hole if something was seen," replied Zarhavar.

"Where is Pelucia in relation to this star-way?" asked Alyssia.

"We will need to take a turn to the right, for the star-way should go all the way to Achernar as you know," answered Zarhavar.

The view ahead of them became brighter, with a blue-green light.

"That's the star of Menkat!" said Zarhavar, "I don't know how bad the star-way route is disrupted where the junction happens. I will get an estimation of it when we get nearer."

The group returned to examine set three of the cards.
"Balancing heaven and earth should be very stabilising," commented Karin.
"Even though we aren't on a planet!" commented Sarah.
Soon they had the set of cards placed under the crystals on top of the other two sets, and helped the crystals to project the images and energies of the cards for the designated half hour. Later, the tannoy came to their attention.
"Well done everyone!" announced Zarhavar, "the spaceship has speeded up even more, by half as much again, so we are making good time. Come through and have more to eat and then relax."

"Are you sure you'd like to do another set after the meal?" asked Zarhavar.
"Yes," replied Hudlath, "we're all agreed aren't we!" and he turned to acknowledge the group, who affirmed that they wished to proceed.
"Definitely," said Costillo.
"If it will help the ship speed up even more, and we have the energy, then we'll do it now!" responded Sarah.
"That's excellent," replied Zarhavar, smiling happily, "ah! Here comes the food!"
An hour or two later after the meal, the group finally emerged from the projection room, and came over to Zarhavar.
"We have definitely spent our energy now!" declared Hudlath.
"My friends, that fourth set of 'linking to the stars' has really boosted the speed, and is allowing us to connect to our own planetary systems now, a great asset, thank you all," said Zarhavar, warmly looking at everyone, "I estimate that we shall be approaching the junction of the Pelucian arm of the star-way in about four or five hours, meanwhile, I'll ascertain how to negotiate it now, because after the other two code sets, the ship will speed up even more."
Zarhavar concentrated a moment, looking at the controls.
"What would you all like to do now? Rest or go to our recreation room and drink our revitalising liquid?" he asked.
Everyone looked at each other. Some said try the liquid and others said they'd prefer to rest.
"I wish to try the liquid," said Alyssia, "coming, girls?"

"Why don't you bring me some, I feel tired out!" answered Sarah.

"Me too, on both accounts!" replied Karin.

"I will," said Alyssia.

Karin and Sarah wandered back to their room and the others went to the recreation facilities.

Hudlath was the first to take a beaker and fill it up. He took a mouthful and swallowed it.

"It's sparkling, but without that carbonated feeling!" he exclaimed.

"Look! It's almost iridescent!" cried Alyssia.

"It definitely restores your energy," said Costillo, "amazing stuff!"

"They definitely don't need any!" chuckled Hudlath, looking at the elves.

"I don't see why not! We have to maintain our superior energy level!" cried Galen.

"Well! If that's the case, we'll let you three do the last code while we rest!" responded Hudlath.

Galen looked for a moment and then his face broke into a broad smile.

"He can't think of a quick enough reply!" said Costillo.

Galen began a jovial bout of shadow boxing for a few moments against Costillo and Hudlath. Alyssia laughed at the three of them, and left with her three glasses of the sparkling elixir.

"Here you are girls! Elixir time!" cried Alyssia at the door.

Sarah opened up and they all took a beaker each and reclined on their beds, sipping the drink.

"Marvellous! I can feel the energy returning to me already!" gasped Karin.

"I know, I can hardly believe it's happening!" replied Sarah.

"It certainly is quite something!" added Alyssia.

"Did either of you find those card sets quite an experience? There wasn't time to ask each other, was there?" asked Karin.

"That's true, it was certainly a crash course in inner work," replied Sarah.

"Having brought the cards through initially, I had already gone through my experiences," commented Alyssia.

"Can you describe them?" asked Karin.

"Yes, when I was feeling disorientated, it was as if all my past lives were being evoked by the energies of the cards, but at the same time, apart from being catalysts, they were also resolving, and helped to conclude the past lives too. It was something in the energy of the cards that did it. The first set began proceedings, the second set continued on and the third set were creating conclusions," explained Alyssia.

"Yes, that's how it appeared to me, and the stability of the cards came about through not only their shape and design, but as a link in a timeless way to footholds of ancient civilisations and cultures," commented Sarah.

"Yes, I especially liked the third set because it offered conclusions by linking the higher and lower chakras," said Karin.

"The fourth set seemed to hint of life beyond earth, where we had been before earthly incarnations, and a sense of subtle inner resolving to be done to make peace with that even more distant past," said Alyssia.

"I had a feeling of that too," mused Sarah, "as if I'd behaved like an unpleasant alien from a sci-fi movie at times, did you?" The others smiled half-apologetically.

"Me too," they both replied.

"You know, I'm beginning to feel a deep peace settle in, as a result of these cards," said Sarah.

"It began once I had the codes downloaded, ever so gradually," replied Alyssia.

"You're right," responded Karin, "with all the concentration on projection I hadn't noticed it, and I feel a deep peace in the heart."

"It's very impressive!" said Sarah, "by the way, how long is it until the next session?"

"I suppose when Zarhavar can get us to wake up again!" said Karin, jovially.

"I seem to remember three hours from when we stopped, so maybe we can expect two hours sleep," commented Alyssia.

"Let's get cracking then!" yawned Sarah, "despite that lovely liquid I still need to get some sleep!"

"Ok, goodnight, or whatever it is!" said Alyssia.

"Good intergalactic intermission, to be correct!" responded Karin.

"And the same to you!" chimed the others, and the light was switched off.

Zarhavar and the accompanying Andromedan ship continued their course with the projected light illuminating and making the way ahead stable. The two ship commanders, Zarhavar and Sirankal mentally communicated with each other.

"Are you sure you can stay with us all the way?" asked Zarhavar.

"Yes, our mission to join other ships in a far area of the next galaxy has been postponed for a while longer," replied Sirankal.

"What is the mission about?" asked Zarhavar.

"We were going to help evacuate the population of that world temporarily, as the planet's volcanic activity would mean an end to life if they remained," explained Sirankal.

"Would they be able to return again?" asked Zarhavar.

"Oh yes, after two or three weeks, whatever the time period, it will be reasonably short," said Sirankal.

"What if they have explosions all of a sudden, right now, unexpectedly?" asked Zarhavar, "for these things aren't easily predictable."

"Yes I know, we've thought of that," replied Sirankal, "but we can tell on this planet as there are many devas who can modify the processes temporarily a bit more than on some worlds."

"Is that because the humanoid inhabitants on the planet aren't on the physical plane?" asked Zarhavar.

"Yes, they aren't, but are there to assist the devic kingdom in their tasks. It's the many creatures that are in need of assistance, for they are still on the physical level," commented Sirankal.

I suspect that planet is phasing out of material existence, then?" asked Zarhavar, "I've known of it, and have watched the beauty of dying stars, but not witnessed this aspect."

"Yes, little by little," replied Sirankal, "you'll find different planets have their own variation on it, but the principle remains the same."

"Are the healer planets still working well in the far reaches?" asked Zarhavar.

"Yes, very well indeed!" replied Sirankal.

Hudlath and Costillo entered at that point and approached Zarhavar.

"I couldn't help overhearing about the healer planets, Zarhavar, where are they situated?" asked Hudlath.

"As you know, they tend to be well interspersed throughout any galaxy, but there also many to be found on the borderline between two galaxies, to ensure that karmic and inter-dimensional forces are properly maintained at these borders," explained Sirankal, "because one galaxy may be at a higher vibrationary rate than the other.

128

"So that the Lords of karma and other wise counsellors live on these planets too, as well as the 'high seat' planetary systems as we call it," asked Hudlath.

"That's true, absolutely!" smiled Sirankal.

"Now!" exclaimed Zarhavar, "would you and your friends like something to eat before resuming with the fifth card set, which will complete operations?"

"Indeed!" responded Hudlath, "Costillo, I'll let the others know!"

Zarhavar put out his hand to halt Hudlath in his tracks.

"You don't need to do anything. I'll wake them with the tannoy!" he gestured.

The fifth card set was soon under way, and the bright energy from their outstretched eagles wings designs soared with strident intent along the star-way ahead of their spaceship. Zarhavar gave voice to the spaceship's increased speed once more, and after an hour the group dispersed, leaving the crystals to continue operations for a while. Hudlath went to see Zarhavar at the helm.

"When do we disengage from this star-way to reach Pelucia?" he asked.

"It won't be long now," replied Zarhavar, and his eyes narrowed and he looked intently towards the far horizon, "I think I see something far ahead, Hudlath, it may be the junction point to Pelucia, and is similar to the one we encountered on the way to the Pleiades."

"Will we need to take precautionary measures?" asked Hudlath.

"Not necessarily now, as the energy build up has been increased dramatically, so all will be well in that stage of the journey," explained Zarhavar.

"Is the planet in question far from that junction?" asked Hudlath.

"To be honest, I don't know how far exactly as yet, but I estimate that it won't be more than an hour's journey," replied Zarhavar.

He then pressed a button and spoke to someone in another part of the ship, "have you mapped where exactly Pelucia is yet?"

Zarhavar turned to look at Hudlath, "my colleagues are just finalising details on Pelucia's precise location, and won't be moment or two in informing me!"

129

"Good, I'll tell the others to come with me, to see you and hear the latest news," replied Hudlath.

"If you all prefer to relax in your rooms, I can tannoy it through to you," responded Zarhavar, "you'll be planning your approach no doubt, but my colleagues are also collecting information on the terrain, and hope to view what's going on there once we get nearer."

"Good, thank you very much Zarhavar," replied Hudlath, "I'll tell the others!"

Hudlath waved amicably and then strode off to the living quarters.

Everyone was gathered together in Sarah, Alyssia and Karin's room, for there was a generous amount of seating in each of the rooms, as well as the beds. After they had been there for an hour, the tannoy gave out its familiar chiming tone and Zarhavar spoke.

"My friends! We are getting quite near to Pelucia. We already have our shield up, so that the ship and the illumined star-way cannot be seen from afar, but we must inform you of the next procedures, so please come and see me now to discuss matters in depth," announced Zarhavar.

The group walked through and gathered round Zarhavar, and three of his crew were present. Sirankal had returned to the Andromedan space ship.

"Please observe this map, it has been charted via our seers using laser crystals. It shows the layout of the buildings there and they have pinpointed where Maraya is being held, and anticipate that she will be moved out of the building briefly at a specific time," instructed Zarhavar, "the tricky part is that we must silence our minds entirely because these beings are telepathic as well, and will become instantly suspicious if they hear us. So, no thoughts throughout operations! If information needs to be given, there are these electronic devices to contact each other and myself."

Zarhavar handed out small pocket-sized devices, not unlike mobile phones, and the group tried them out.

"As you can see, there are standard phrases for difficult situations, like 'I am being attacked', or 'we need more personnel for this job," explained Zarhavar, "we can input other required phrases, so that if the occasion occurs you would press the activation button to notify us. What do you suggest to add?"

Zarhavar looked questioningly around at everyone.

" 'We see Maraya, but can't reach her', or 'we have Maraya with us but are being attacked and need more help'," suggested Costillo.

"Good, I will add the phrases and then I will link up the machines so the information is then in all of them," said Zarhavar.

"If any unexpected problems occur," suggested Hudlath; "then I'd have to manually text it through to you!"

"Yes, let's hope it doesn't happen!" replied Zarhavar.

There was a moment of silence as people pondered seriously on the job in hand, and then Zarhavar spoke again.

"The atmosphere is very dark on Pelucia and the whole planet is surrounded by a viscous and dense layer, so we will simply raise the energy of the ship and everyone on board to become more subtle, in order to slip through easier. We will then swoop down and catch Maraya up in our magnetic field, and if you, Costillo and who else wishes to help? Yes, Hudlath! Both of you could be ready in the transporter room to receive her safely into the ship. Two of the crew will help you put on safety outfits, and they will wear them too, in case she has any trouble in being picked up."

"What kind of trouble could occur?" asked Costillo, frowning with concern.

"She may be lifted up, but not quite reach the aperture as we pass by, but you could venture out of the ship with those outfits, which have cords attached to the ship. There are additional cord attachments on the outfits, which are to be unzipped out of a side pocket, which can be used to 'lasso' Maraya to safely bring her in," advised Zarhavar.

"Right! I understand," replied Costillo, "when do we start?"

"We're going to enter the Pelucian atmosphere very shortly, so please go to the transporter room. The crew will prepare you, and notify me when you're ready," said Zarhavar.

"Let's go!" said Costillo to Hudlath.

They turned to everyone and gave a determined smile, then swiftly departed.

"Is there anything we can do?" asked the others.

"If you three ladies could go to the projection room, we'll need your extra input once we are on the point of leaving Pelucia," replied Zarhavar, "as for the three elves," and Zarhavar glanced briefly as Alyssia, Sarah and Karin departed, "I'll need your help to ensure that our crystals all over the ship will withstand the Pelucian atmosphere. It's terribly draining. I'll show you a plan of where they're housed, so you could input a top up to their energy levels as much as you can."

Zarhavar pressed a button on another screen to reveal a plan view of the ship, and then another press of a button to show a mass of flashing lights where all the crystals were housed.

"The large one at centre is the most important, if you could go there and keep that one charged throughout our stay in Pelucia's atmosphere, that would be excellent. With any luck we won't be longer than half an hour," explained Zarhavar, "one of the crew will assist you, inform me when you get there and then we can begin."

The elves departed and Zarhavar waited by the controls. After a few minutes the affirmative responses came from Costillo and Hudlath, and also the elves.

Zarhavar looked at his crew members with slight apprehension. He then raised his hand to them and nodded, so that they all used the controls to raise the vibratory level of the ship, and a mass of bright energy filled it, bringing more peace as a result. Then he pressed the control lever, which began the ship's silent descent towards the dark, smoky atmosphere below.

Chapter 9 – The Crystalline Planet of Healing

Karin, Alyssia and Sarah's view from the projection room, like other viewing platforms, was obliterated by that black, oily layer which was an efficient barrier for any escape routes. With the heightening of the ship's energetic levels, it slipped through the morass easily. Some kind of structure became briefly visible to the girls, and they looked at each other with curiosity, which swiftly turned to horror as they realised it was the remnants of a space ship that had been caught in the cloying web.

The ship gradually descended into a twilight world of perpetual gloom. Here and there were lights, and the girls spied small spacecraft moving around, but were not suitable for travelling far afield however. At the helm, Zarhavar checked on a video screen near to Karin's crystal, where Jadeir and Kenny had given their last message to the group. An image of the elves could be seen avidly concentrating on bringing through a continuous supply of extra energy. He then checked a dial, which indicated that energy levels were satisfactory, and then he steered the ship further downwards, knowing that they wouldn't be so detectable at their present frequency. He pressed a knob on the helm's console and a series of co-ordinates came up on the viewing window, with coloured lights down the edge. Zarhavar's group of seers had given accurate coordinates, and he knew that when all the coloured lights on the control panel were green, he would be in the exact area to intercept Maraya. He also knew that there were any further developments, a group of red lights would start flashing, and would link him directly to the transporter room.

Meanwhile, in the transporter room, Hudlath and Costillo had donned their outfits and the aperture at floor level was beginning to open, revealing the dark smoky atmosphere below. The crew member was viewing another smaller screen version of the co-ordinates as to where Maraya would be, and also awaited the lights to all simultaneously turn green. Hudlath and Costillo peered through the aperture into Pelucia's twilit world and saw the ground and its accompanying signs of habitation come gradually closer. 200 feet, 150 feet, 100 feet ……… 50 feet, then the green lights flashed dramatically. The crew member swiftly started up the light rays that would lift Maraya upwards. The light descended downwards as the ship still lowered itself, and then the light touched ground. A helmeted figure was lifted upwards, and then two more got caught in the beam and ascended. Hudlath and Costillo stood at the edge; ready to apprehend the first figure, hoping it was Maraya. The being came up through the aperture, and Hudlath caught hold of an arm and brought the figure over. Hudlath briefly peered in the visor, and indicated that it wasn't Maraya, but by then the being was defiantly demanding to be let go of, and tried to assault Hudlath, but he had a crystal to hand, and made the being unconscious and placed him to one side. Meanwhile, the other two beings were coming up. Costillo grabbed one and that one began fighting too, but the third proved to be Maraya, and Hudlath let out an involuntary sound, so everyone knew. The crew member placed the light rays into reverse mode, and indicated to the others to put the two characters over the edge and they'd be safely lowered back to ground. Costillo managed to push the Pelucian over the edge while Hudlath dragged the first one and rolled him over.

Once done, the aperture was closed, and the crew member pressed an affirmative signal to the helm, and the ship moved speedily upwards, and cleared the black barrier in minutes. They all removed their space suits and Maraya removed her helmet. Costillo looked at her, holding her face in his hands and then hugged her tightly. They all went to the bridge to see Zarhavar. Then Alyssia, Sarah and Karin came rushing through from the projector room to see Maraya, and they all hugged her in turn.
"I hope that the atmosphere there hasn't undermined your health too much Maraya," commented Sarah.
"I know, it was impossible to breathe for long, and we were allowed to put on those helmets most of the time. But the awful thing was, that there were always too few helmets there, as they tended to deteriorate quite quickly in that atmosphere, and so those who didn't get one usually died after a day of inhalation," explained Maraya.
"What did you have to do every day, Maraya?" asked Costillo.
"We had to help in the construction of new buildings, digging foundations, sawing and the usual type of chores, and no one could escape doing it, and they worked you hard with little to eat," replied Maraya.
"What kind of food did you have?" asked Karin.
"I don't want to remember," uttered Maraya quietly.

Her face became ashen and everyone crowded round making sympathetic noises.

"I'm so sorry Maraya," exclaimed Karin, holding her hand.

Zarhavar gave Maraya a concerned look.

"I think we'd better give you a proper medical check, Maraya, and also a course of our specialised foods to make you healthy again."

He contacted the crew via the tannoy and a medical style trolley arrived with healing crystals glowing all over it. Zarhavar, Hudlath and Costillo helped Maraya onto the trolley as she had become quite giddy.

"Don't worry Maraya, you're just feeling a reaction from having endured the Pelucian atmosphere, along with everything else," said Zarhavar, "but we'll get you back to good health."

She was wheeled away, and the others left Costillo to go with her initially, so the two of them could have some time together.

As the others went off to eat a light meal, Zarhavar approached the junction onto the main star-way route, which ran on towards Achernar. He contacted the Andromedan ship.

"Sirankal! Are you ready to cut off the diverting route?" asked Zarhavar.

"I certainly am!" Sirankal replied.

"When I give you the word, we start……..now!" Zarhavar almost shouted.

The ships were both hovering over the star-way junction, and a fiery mass of strong energy descended from the ships and began dissolving the diversion route until there was nothing left, and there was only the star-way route continuing on to Achernar with no interruptions. The two space ships made to set off, when something appeared from Pelucia. It was one of the small space ships, which had managed to venture through the black barrier. Zarhavar turned with surprise on seeing it approaching.

"Sirankal! Do you see what I see?" asked Zarhavar.

"I do! I'll use the detractor ray to stop the ship's advance," Sirankal replied.

The result was like a wall of flame and then after it faded, the Pelucian ship tried to advance again, but hit an invisible wall, which had now surrounded the whole of Pelucia as well.

"Well and truly trapped now!" responded Zarhavar.

"Absolutely!" replied Sirankal, "do you need any further assistance?"

"Well, no I don't think so now," replied Zarhavar, thank you very much for your help Sirankal."

"Glad to be of service," replied Sirankal, "I think I'll continue to Achernar and ensure the star-way is pristine again."

"Oh good, as Maraya needs some recuperation, so we'll have to visit the healing planet of the Pylon of Phairos," replied Zarhavar, "and we shall undo the knot near the Pleiades."

"Excellent! Then our ship can return to Andromeda," replied Sirankal, "goodbye!"

The sound of his goodbye resounded throughout Zarhavar's ship, so that everyone heard it simultaneously, and he received a chorus of replies from everyone by return.

"I wonder how Maraya is faring?" asked Sarah, articulating everyone else's thoughts.

"It beats me how she managed to survive on such a contagious planet, it must have been almost like living at the bottom of a tar pit," replied Karin.

"Yes, even with a helmet," responded Alyssia.

"Let's go and see Hudlath and the elves," announced Sarah, "come on!"

She got up from the couch in their room, and the other two followed. They wandered round to Hudlath's room and knocked on his door.

"No answer!" said Sarah.

"I'll try the elves," cried Alyssia, and she half ran to their door and knocked, "funny! No reply again!"

"Ok, let's go and see Zarhavar," said Karin.

They all hastily proceeded to the helm, and were relieved to see Zarhavar there.

"Oh Zarhavar! Where is everyone?" asked Karin.

"Is Maraya all right?" questioned Alyssia.

"All is fine! Don't worry yourselves," replied Zarhavar, "Hudlath and the elves are with Maraya and Costillo, and are helping to stabilise her condition too, as her system, as you can understand, needs to be healed at a deep cellular level after that experience. It was her determination to escape that kept her going, but once she was safe, there a sudden lapse of her whole system."

"I do hope she will recuperate soon," said Sarah, with a worried expression on her face.

"Yes she will, we are speedily returning, and should approach the junction point quite soon. Your assistance would be appreciated in the projector room. I'll tell you what to do, and the idea is to just project energy at the ties between the two star-ways, rather than the removal of one of them as in the previous occasion."

"Certainly Zarhavar," replied Sarah.

"We'll go now!" responded Karin, "come on, girls!"

The three of them departed towards the room in question and approached the crystal stands. The tannoy sang out and Zarhavar spoke.

"If you three could activate all the crystals, asking them to work, and while concentrating on one each during the star-way operation, to encourage the other crystals to follow what your own crystal is doing. It will work! I shall leave you to talk to the other crystals, having chosen the ones you intend to work with, and I shall talk to you once action is required," explained Zarhavar.

"Let's get chatting!" said Sarah.

"Why don't we take arrange ourselves so that one is at the central crystal, and the other two at either end of the row, and we can talk to the ones nearest us?" suggested Alyssia.

"Sounds good to me," remarked Karin.

They began talking to the crystals next to the ones they had chosen, and projected some energy via the crystals to encourage the others to link in.

"I think they've realised what we're on about," said Sarah.

"Yes, I'm sure they'd know something instantly. It's simply a question of trying to convey it non-verbally, which is hard," responded Karin.

"Not a difficulty to an artist!" replied Alyssia.

"Ah! We'll know who to ask in future!" remarked Sarah.

"Oh look! I think I can see something ahead," announced Karin.

They all looked at the viewing screen. Through the illuminated tunnel of the star-way, the crossover of the Pleiadean star-way could be seen, for the walls of the star-way were semi-transparent. It would take about ten minutes to reach it, estimated by the speed they were travelling at. As anticipated, the tannoy announced itself and Zarhavar spoke.

"As you can see, the Pleiadean star-way approaches. We have a new plan now. I've been in touch with the Pleiadean command, who, in turn contacted the Aurigan and Achernar domains, as we have decided to link the two star-ways together properly, and in moments there will be ships coming from all three star groups," he explained, "and we may still be required to help, but I shall communicate with them first and find out procedures. As you know, the priority is to get to the Pylon of Phairos."

Sure enough, three spaceships approached, and the third was from behind them. After a period of negotiation, Zarhavar talked again to Sarah and the others.

"It has been decided upon to open up the star-way to improve communication by creating more inter-linking routes between the various star-ways, so that there is less chance of the hijacking of planets and star-ways happening. Once we have finished work near the Pleiades, we intend to take an interconnection between the Pleiadean star-way at a point not far from Rigel, and connecting it up with Sirius," explained Zarhavar, "and that's only one of the star-way connections!" and he half chuckled.

"How many connecting points do you have in mind?" asked Sarah.

"We'll find out when everyone meets up, then we shall have a conferring of ideas," replied Zarhavar.

"Zarhavar," asked Karin, "isn't Sirius linked with us already, like the other council of twelve members' planets?"

"Oh yes, but indirectly, the star routes have been a very basic network, but as we can travel very quickly, we didn't think they needed to have extra networking, but now it is thought necessary," explained Zarhavar.

"Apart from the security reason, do you think it is so that Sirius can have a greater influence on Earth?" asked Alyssia.

Zarhavar gave Alyssia an astute look. "There's a grain of truth in that question, and I shall explain soon, but now the ships are arriving," replied Zarhavar hurriedly, and gave them all a smile.

"Come aboard everyone!" he announced to the three ships.

Immediately a representative from Achernar, Auriga and the Pleiades entered their room.

"I am Valdan!" said the one from Achernar, who looked remarkably like an Earth inhabitant, but was tall and slim with a long aquiline face, and bright lustrous eyes of a pale peach colour.

"I am Deran," said the Aurigan, whose skin was pale and faintly opalescent, and there was a strange musical air to be discerned, which became apparent just after he had spoken.

"And I am Saldan," said the Pleiadean warmly. His skin was dark blue, like many other Pleiadeans.

The three of them and Zarhavar looked at each other intently, wordlessly communicating for a few minutes. It was as if the introduction was purely a show for the others. They shook hands again and the three departed back to their spaceships. Zarhavar turned to face Alyssia, Sarah and Karin.

"My friends, we shall wait here until the star-way junction has been fixed, but if you three could go to the projector room, because a blessing of the star-way's junction is in order!"

"Certainly!" cried Karin, and the others smiled.

They walked briskly to the projector room and settled by the crystals, awaiting instructions. They could see the construction in progress. The junction points were dissolved by a flash of white light from each of the spaceships, and then blue light was sent, which aligned the star-ways together, and the star-way walls were filled in and completed.

"They did it so quickly!" cried Alyssia in amazement, "could you imagine a motorway being built as fast as that?"

"No!" came the reply from the other two.

The tannoy sang out once more.

"Please send out the energy now!" announced Zarhavar.

The energy surged out from the crystals, travelling down the star-way to the junction, and filled it with masses of light. It became radiant and a blue shimmer surrounded it.

"All is well now, you can stop!" said Zarhavar.

Their spaceship progressed as the three others departed, and they entered the junction. Once inside, they could see something filling the area.

"Look at that!" cried Karin.

"It's beautiful!" cried Alyssia, wishing she had her sketchbook.

"Yes, but does anyone know what it is?" asked Sarah, transfixed.

Karin looked at the three intersecting circles of light that were rotating individually, and as a group too, which generated a bluish light continuously.

"Perhaps it is there to act as a guardian energy and stop infiltration," ventured Karin.

"Yes, I agree," said Alyssia, "and perhaps the symbol is of the universe, since it is comprised of atomic structural shapes."

"Thank you girls, I could go along with that," replied Sarah.

She continued to look at it with wonder and fascination as the others did. Once they had passed by and realised that Zarhavar had turned left into the Pleiadean to Earth star-way, they came out of their reverie and wandered back to see Zarhavar.

"That star-way junction energy was breathtaking," commented Sarah.

"Yes indeed, it will ensure all is well now with the star-ways, and many more will be put in as the junctions are created," he said.

The bright lights of Taurus came into view, and Zarhavar placed the ship on emergency speed, and soon the light shining from Rigel came and went, and then they were fast approaching the Pylon of Phairos. Zarhavar spoke in his tannoy.

"Attention everyone! We are approaching the Pylon of Phairos. Prepare to land!" he cried, "the planet in question is called Pharon."

Alyssia, Sarah and Karin clicked their seatbelts into position, knowing that Hudlath, the elves, Maraya and Costillo would be doing the same in the healing room, along with the crew members. The bright shining group of stars were well in view, and everyone was transfixed by the beauty of this star group. Each star shone brilliant white light with bright sparkles intermittently. In the centre was a cluster of planets.

"There's the planet Pharias that Jaysangar is on," remarked Zarhavar.

The opalescent atmosphere surrounding the planet in question came into view, which made everyone feel extremely peaceful.

"Is this the planet we are going to?" asked Sarah.

"No, it is the one next to it, which has all the crystals," replied Zarhavar.

There was a sound of crackling, and Kenny's face appeared on the screen, with Jadeir beside him.

"Hey! We can see them again!" he exclaimed excitedly, then his face looked more serious, "Karin, is Maraya aboard?"

"Yes, she's in the healing room, but she'll be fine," replied Karin.

"What a relief!" and Kenny exhaled and visibly relaxed, "When will you return home?" asked Kenny.

"We have to take Maraya to a healing planet on the Pylon of Phairos, and then we will be able to return, but can't give you any details as yet, time wise, but will keep you informed," replied Karin.

"Very well, dear, goodbye for now," replied Kenny, and their faces faded away.

The planet in question was surrounded in a layer of golden light and exuded an aura of deep peace, like Pharias. There were exclamations of delight from the group. Especially when the ship gently descended through an iridescent indigo layer, which, despite the deep hue, was charged with a bright light of its own, and there were golden sparkles, some of which formed into spirals, the aum sign, six pointed stars, amongst many shapes.

"It's like floating through a gaseous form of lapis lazuli," cried Alyssia.

"I couldn't have put it better myself," responded Sarah.

The layer of indigo gradually changed to peacock blue, with flecks of crystalline light, and then to a pale duck egg hue, and soon the planet itself came into view.

"Will you look at that!" cried Sarah.

"My goodness, it's beyond the word beautiful!" exclaimed Alyssia.

They all got up and wandered over to the viewing windows. In the healing room, Maraya was being assisted to her motorised wheelchair, and they made their way to the transporter room.

"Come along everyone! Time to disembark!" announced Zarhavar, smiling at their reverie, "the view affects everyone like this!"

They left the helm and met Maraya, Costillo, Hudlath and the elves at the end of the first corridor. Zarhavar ushered them all towards the exit where they descended a ramp by the side of the transporter room. Once outside the ship, the group were transfixed again at the view. The peacock blue sky shimmered with an iridescent sheen over amethyst quartz topped mountains, which had large opalescent crystals interspersed.

"I never thought I'd see amethyst crystal mountains like this!" remarked Sarah, looking completely amazed.

"Those opalescent white crystals are what fascinate me," said Karin, "I'd love to see one up close."

"Magnificent!" cried Alyssia.

"Follow me, everyone and you'll see the lot close up!" exclaimed Zarhavar, moving off towards the mountains in question.

The three ladies started following Zarhavar, with Hudlath behind, and Costillo was walking closely beside Maraya, who was moving along in her wheelchair. Zarhavar turned around and pointed at Maraya's wheelchair, and it began to rise up slowly until it was about three inches off the ground.

141

"Just ask it to go forward, and it will do so," explained Zarhavar, smiling slightly at Maraya's surprised expression; "the path becomes a bit uneven in places."

Maraya asked Costillo something very briefly, and mainly through sign language.

"Maraya is asking how you get it to hover?" queried Costillo.

"I link to the energetic source of Pharon's planetary core, and then ask for the gravitational effect to be lessened by a degree. That's the basis of it!" explained Zarhavar.

He then pointed to a cave entrance in the mountainside ahead of them to where the pathway was leading them.

"We are going to that cave!" he uttered.

A deep violet glow was visible once they had entered, and there was a very faint perfume, like the residual smell of incense or essential oil having been used in a room. There was a lovely peaceful atmosphere there, and a large sofa became apparent to them. It was also the same colour, and lined the whole length of the wall. All except Zarhavar and Maraya were on the sofa. The light went to such a deep violet, that everyone couldn't see each other. Then a white opalescent energy began to pulsate slowly in three places around them. They felt a surge of energy and deep peace come to them, and they wallowed in a euphoric state for some moments.

"Welcome, my friends!" came a gentle female voice.

Everyone brought themselves round to a more alert state, to see a tall being dressed in a white opalescent robe, smiling to them. The still near-recumbent group smiled back.

"My name is Eldina, please come with me and we can help your friend," she said.

They moved to a lift, which ascended to the apex of the mountain's interior, and arrived at a light and airy room, of which the walls were made of pure crystal, amethyst and the white opalescent ones. Light shone through a very thin layer of tiny crystals overhead.

"I know you have amethyst on your planet, but the white ones are called Opalestra, and are only found here. Come, Maraya, let us get you on this crystal bed," said Eldina.

Eldina activated the crystals under the floor, which had been covered in a very thick glass-like substance. They began to glow and Maraya was lifted up and gently placed on the crystal bed, which then also began to glow. Eldina gently tended to her to ensure she was comfortable, and put a blanket over her.

"We shall leave you here for a while," said Eldina to Maraya, and she paused in thought momentarily, "for two or three hours in your time," and she looked at the Oswestry group especially. "Please go into the adjacent room, for it may be of interest to you!" then she turned to Maraya again, "we shall not be far away, and I shall know if you need me from wherever I am in this mountainside," and she smiled to Maraya.

The others all filed through, and Eldina followed them.
Everyone stopped in their tracks, transfixed yet again, except Zarhavar, who knew all about it. Even Hudlath was very impressed, and he had done some travelling in space. There seemed to be nothing but crystals around them, glowing very brightly, so that the colour was a paler violet, with the usual Opalestra light, which shone here with an especial pearly glow, and an opalescent sheen. The light was pulsating very slowly. Eldina came into the room, paused for a few moments and then asked them to follow her further along the room, and kept on walking. Everyone looked at each other as if to say, 'where is the end of this room!' She continued to walk along until, after several minutes, they came to a small spiral staircase cut carefully into the crystal, so that not too many of the amethysts were disrupted.

Once they reached the top, they saw the room was circular, like the healing room below, except that the walls only came up to shoulder height, and a beautiful glass dome was upon the top, encrusted here and there with Opalestra crystal clusters. They could all gain a magnificent view of the crystalline planet from the highest peak of the mountaintop.
"What function does this room hold, Eldina?" asked Karin.
"It is a meditation room, you might say, and there are other purposes," she added, a little enigmatically, "please arrange yourselves into a circle, and I shall show you a little of what I mean."
Once in position, they all assumed a meditative silence, with attention at the third eye. The others were unaware that Eldina was hovering around, so as to not disturb everyone, and placed her attention on the Opalestra crystals in the glass dome, which were about six inches in diameter. A strange filmy substance came from them and hung down about a foot below the crystals. Eldina pulled on one of them and drew it downwards over Karin, who was just below, and draped it

around her, and then did the same for all the others. She then returned to her place, bringing the substance around her too. The atmosphere changed, bringing in more light and a sense of atmic no time that dazzled everyone.

Alyssia felt herself floating up out of her body, and noticed everyone else doing the same, hovering just above their bodies. They smiled at each other and Eldina beckoned them upwards, out of the dome. She pointed to a magnificent mountain that was much higher than the rest. They all flew speedily towards the mountain in question, which had a ring of golden mist around it. Eldina directed them all to a ledge about two-thirds up the side facing them. They then landed and moved along until a small cave entrance was visible, and filed inside.

After the momentary darkness and confinement of a narrow and small entranceway, a door opened to find a huge room, filled with glorious light, so bright that everyone had to stop and adjust themselves to it. The air was filled with many gold and iridescent patterns like moiré effect, Indian carpet designs and intricate leaf shapes, and so on, and everything had a light of its own. Greetings came from somewhere amidst the swirling patterns to the group. Eldina took them across the room to a large circular well in the centre, which, they realised was naturally formed by volcanic activity when the planet was very young, and the hot springs subsequent to that had been stronger flowing and would have washed through the whole room for many, many centuries.

Beside the well were another three tall beings like Eldina, also with white opalescent robes. Their faces looked slightly older, and their eyes danced with an opal-tinged light. They beckoned the group to come over and drink. Eldina took some of the water for Maraya in a sealable container. Alyssia drank some of the water, which sparkled and fizzed. She felt herself ascending up the shaft of light to the top of the mountain. Up there was a dome of light too, and she could see linking light-shafts to the suns of the Pylon of Phairos, with huge fiery beings who moved around, working to keep energy flowing. Alyssia just 'knew' about how they linked energy-wise to Taurus and other planets and systems around, and also a sense of the planet's history. She floated back down and the others took their turns, while she went over to Eldina.

"There aren't many people living here, Eldina, why aren't there more?" she asked.

"We don't live like on your planet, hundreds and thousands of people very close together. There are about eighty people on this planet, and many work in making objects of use, teaching, temple building, and, of course, healing those on ours and other planets. We are happy with that and don't need to live in such a physical way as your Earth population does," replied Eldina.

"That sounds very reasonable to me, a smaller population would be healthier and much less stressed, especially when spiritually aligned and not so materially involved," answered Alyssia.

"Yes, we do not need to forage for food, as we get our sustenance from this well, and the light energy, and occasionally some fruits, which we grow in the great valley to the west, the other side of this mountain," explained Eldina.

When all the others had ascended the light shaft and returned, the group took their leave of the three beings at the well, and waved goodbye to them. Eldina then took them to the entrance again, and they left, speeding towards the dome in the mountaintop, and then returned into their bodies, and came out of the meditation.

After a moment's re-adjustment, Eldina went to visit Maraya, asking the others to come when they were ready. Zarhavar arose first and then Hudlath, followed by the others shortly after. When they came through to the healing room, there was a deep blue glow around Maraya, and she was awake and smiling at Eldina.

"You will be fine now, Maraya, but you can take an Opalestra with you to maintain yourself within the first two weeks, but you'll find you won't really need it for long," advised Eldina, and she turned to look at the others, "I do have pieces for all of you too, as I always give some away, for I know it is so beneficial for people, and we are fortunate on this planet, for the crystals grow back very quickly, so there's an endless supply."

They said farewell to Eldina and could see her energy field glow with violet and gold. Maraya was able to walk back to the space ship as normal, and Zarhavar made the wheelchair rise up and float back to the ship by itself. Once inside, Zarhavar executed lift off, and whilst seated, everyone could view the beautiful layers of the planet's atmosphere again. The ship passed through the last part of the indigo, and then the golden layer. The seatbelts could now be released and so everyone got up.

"Homeward bound now!" said Zarhavar, cheerfully, and he smiled at the group.

"I'm so glad you're back to normal, Maraya," said Sarah, giving Maraya a hug.

"Thank you Sarah, I'm feeling really good," replied Maraya.

"And the same from us!" said Karin, quickly looking at Alyssia, who affirmed a yes. They both hugged Maraya.

"What were you all doing when I was on that beautiful crystal bed?" asked Maraya.

"Aha!" cried Costillo dramatically, and Maraya looked at him mischievously.

"Maybe you fell asleep on that sofa!" she replied.

Costillo laughed.

"That would have been nice! But Eldina led us to a room next to the healing room full of pale violet glowing crystals, and then went down a corridor to a spiral staircase up into the apex of the mountain, and there we meditated. We then astral travelled to a mountain and had some experiences there!" explained Costillo.

"What kind of experiences, Costillo?" asked Maraya.

Costillo told her about the interior room in the mountain.

"I levitated to the top of the shaft of light and could see more stars and planets than when we were travelling in our physical bodies. The sky was golden for quite a distance around the planet and the stars. There were beings from all these places who came over to me and told me how the universe was made through the purest combination of thought and love, so much love that we'd all be blown away by it, and so much detailed and vast capacity of thought that you'd almost need a universe-sized computer to house it. I just gasped in amazement and wished that I could feel even a better proportion of that to justify my existence," explained Costillo.

"I felt the same," said Alyssia, "but the beings showed me the beauty of different worlds, the other healing planets in the universe, all with crystals, but some were more gentle and loving, while others were more intense, you might say, to bring through strong and vibrant energy, depending on what would be required. I just hope I can remember enough to paint all the images I'd like to when we return."

"I'll look forward to that!" cried Maraya.

"I saw so many beings too, who all seemed to blend together as one being, and then they were separate again," said Karin, "they told me they did that to show how near to unity they are, and they were appealing to us to remove the ego and reach to the God consciousness, and really strive to conquer the little self that limits understanding. They came close to me and tried to convey that feeling of unity, and it was like an acute awareness of all life, with a very deep love of creation and a sure-footed understanding of what tasks to do if incarnated. The feeling was so uplifting, beautiful, and so moving too!"

Karin's eyes began to fill with tears and everyone hugged her.

"I felt a deep love come to me," said Sarah, once everyone had stopped hugging, and looked in anticipation to her experience.

"I only saw one being, like an enormous angel the size of a planet. The being's voice was neither male nor female, and she shone a light towards me and I felt myself going down a tunnel of light though I knew I was still at the mountain top. There was a very dazzling sun that I could hardly look at, and I was taken to a planet nearby upon which were the most spectacular waterfalls, with dazzling displays of crystals, rocks of gold and iridescence unimaginable. There were communities based there, set in beautiful buildings. I just knew it was very harmonious there, and everyone totally worked for the good of all. Somehow, just seeing that and bringing that thought strongly to mind was powerful. The atmosphere was marvellous and healing, for there were no bad thoughts or actions to bring the energy down."

The three elves, Galen, Pireus and Calani drew attention to them-selves now. Pireus was the spokesperson.

"Excuse us, but no-one noticed where we went as we slid off to talk to all the beings of the earth below ground. They were quite similar to the ones on Earth, and it was very enjoyable for the rocks below ground are very beautiful indeed!"

"I have known of this healing planet of Pharon for a long time," said Hudlath, "but wished to join in anyway. I was lifted up, and saw all that everyone else has mentioned. I also saw the historical evolution of Pharon, and the whole of the Pylon of Phairos group. How each star system emanated out of a central point, from what you and I would call the central spiritual sun. It was like a vast cluster of unified thought, love and consciousness, and then all the stars and planets began to move outwards. When this whole universal age period had reached a substantial stage of evolution, all the star systems begin to converge again."

"Amazing!" said Alyssia, while Karin, Sarah and Maraya were paused in thought.

"What did you see, Zarhavar?" asked Hudlath.

"I saw the same as you all," replied Zarhavar, "though I wish to add that, when the universe is converging again, it is doing it from a different place in the universe, so it is not the same as when it was last in a state of convergence. I also saw other universes surrounding ours. They were going through their own cycles at different rates to ours. Some were much quicker, and others slower. Many are very advanced, others just a bit more so than us. I saw the many universes from a plan view, and they looked incredibly beautiful, even the less advanced parts, for the rest of the universe supported them, ensuring that their lack of harmony was held in check. I just felt the glowing love from the centre of the universe rush through me."

With that, Zarhavar's eyes became luminous, and everyone could see his energy fields becoming suffused with gold and white light.

"Zarhavar!" exclaimed Alyssia, "you are more cosmic than I realised!"

Zarhavar turned to look at her and smiled.

"Yes I am really, I just don't boast about it! There is nothing to boast about when you feel deep peace all the time, it is both humbling and wonderful, I am too contented!" he replied.

"Zarhavar, that was illuminating," cried Maraya, "could I ask you how you all managed to get to Pelucia?"

"It's a long story!" replied Zarhavar, "why don't we all relax together and have something to eat. My crew will return us to Earth meanwhile."

"Zarhavar, I'll just call Kenny and let him know we are on our way home now," said Karin.

"Certainly, go ahead Karin," replied Zarhavar.

Zarhavar called a crew member to the helm, and then they retired to a lounge, where two other crew members served them all with some food. They all explained to Maraya about the codes, and how they had been needed to re-activate and lighten the star-way towards Pelucia beyond the Hyades.

"So where did the codes come from?" asked Maraya.

"Well, Alyssia intercepted them, didn't you!" ventured Hudlath.

"Yes! I saw them come into my third eye when I went for a walk up to Old Oswestry hill fort, but I saw your face with some dolphins too," replied Alyssia.

Maraya's face looked thoughtful, and a shadow of puzzlement came into her eyes momentarily, and then she gasped.

"Oh, by the lights of Sirius! I've forgotten that I was on the way to the Pleiades, and yes, the small spaceship I was in," and she paused in thought, "it was heading for – Pelucia. I remember, I had been sucked into the vortex and was encapsulated in energy, which would have guarded me on up the star-way to the Pleiades. I was given the codes from the Pleiades at a planet near Taurus, just beforehand, by a being called Caelina. She said they needed to return to Earth at this time and that I must send them along the star-way to someone reliable, and that I could use a device she had which would project them effectively, as long as I could focus on someone. I thought of you, Alyssia, since you could draw them as well as see them. Then I continued on my way, but I became unconscious somehow and found myself on that spaceship in a very small room on my own."

"So the codes came from the Pleiades!" cried Alyssia, "were they created there?" and she turned to Hudlath and Zarhavar.

"Their true origin was from Sirius, but have been used for such a long time on other planets, and occasionally on Earth, that the original source gets forgotten," explained Zarhavar.

"When was the last time they were used on Earth, my friend?" asked Hudlath.

"When the beings from the Pleiades and Sirius first came to bring good culture and spiritual ways to Earth, in Atlantis and Lemuria," replied Zarhavar, "and now in the time of Anchorin and Hudlath."

"I'm glad you added my name too!" said Hudlath, and everyone laughed.

"Do the codes affect people as well as environments?" asked Maraya.

"Yes they do," answered Alyssia, "there are several sets of codes, but we only used five of them. They work on various levels of your psyche via images for each chakra, dealing with self-transformation in its many layers. Were you not able to see much of the codes before you sent them?"

"Yes, I remember seeing a group of eye shapes, diamonds, six pointed stars and circles, as well as stars with more points on them, things are still coming back to me of those moments before I was captured," replied Maraya.

"Yes, the eye images are the first group called 'Opening up to Spirituality,' and the second group are the diamonds, 'Linking to the Heavenly Light,' where the waking energy is taken a little higher, linking with solar energy. The next is 'Balancing Heaven and Earth,' the hexagonal shapes, and it helps to link up the various chakras in the body to clear up energy and integrate the symbiosis of the chakra system. Group four, 'Linking to the stars' brings in stellar energy and a great deal of peace and light. Group five is 'Linking to Higher Dimensions,' and helps to clear a lot of deeper issues, which keep you in a state of illusion," explained Alyssia, "we were half working on ourselves and out along the star-way!"

"They do sound interesting, I wish I could see them," responded Maraya.

"Certainly Maraya, I shall give you a full pack, and everyone else a pack each too, and an extra one for Anchorin," replied Zarhavar, "which reminds me, we can't be far away from Earth."

With that the tannoy sang out.

"Zarhavar, we are approaching Pluto now!" said the crew member at the helm.

"We'd better get ready and collect our belongings," said Hudlath.

"I'll see you all at the bridge," said Zarhavar.

"Come and see our rooms if you wish, Maraya," cried Karin, putting an arm around her cordially.

They all went off together and soon returned again to see the edge of Jupiter's rings receding away, and Mars coming rapidly closer.

"Will you be coming into Anchorin's temple, Zarhavar?" asked Hudlath.

"Not this time, Hudlath," replied Zarhavar, "I've got a few more destinations to visit. Ah! Aurial and Salodan wish to say goodbye too."

There was a shimmering energy that ran through the ship as Aurial and Salodan came through to the bridge, and they kindly shook hands with everyone.

150

"I see we have just returned to Anchorin's time period!" said Salodan.

"We are sorry we haven't seen much of you all for the journey, but we got diverted by various galactic problems and have been talking with the other planets via our communications centre, which lies at the heart of the ship," explained Aurial.

"We are most grateful for your help with the code projection too," added Salodan, "and we are very grateful for all of you, as well as the crew for helping us to get Maraya back."

"I'm so grateful to you!" cried Maraya, and she gently hugged Aurial, Salodan and Zarhavar.

By this time they could feel the ship descending through the Earth's atmosphere, and coming down towards Anchorin's temple.

"Just go to the transporter room and you'll be able to descend to the temple safely," instructed Zarhavar, "goodbye all, and your cards are waiting for you by the transporter room too!"

They exchanged goodbyes and were all soon inside Anchorin's temple discussing the journey's events, and also the cards.

"Would you like to stay a while or return to Oswestry right now?" asked Anchorin.

"I would love to stay, but I think I'd like to return and see Kenny, if you two don't mind," said Karin, looking at Sarah and Alyssia, then back to Anchorin.

"I'm happy to return now, I'm tired out!" responded Sarah.

"Well, ok, I'll have to say yes too, won't I!" replied Alyssia, smiling, "it's ok for we know we can return any time and visit you all."

By this time, everyone was gathered around to say goodbye again.

"Yes, we would love you to come and visit us," said Costillo, and Maraya smiled broadly to Alyssia, Sarah and Karin.

"I hope you can come and see my new house too!" replied Sarah.

"We'll do that!" answered Costillo.

"We will too!" cried the elves.

Alyssia gave the thumbs up signal, and they departed for Oswestry.

Chapter 10 – The Promise in the Well

Sarah, Karin and Alyssia re-appeared into the healing room downstairs, having returned to Old Oswestry hill fort in the Atlantean aircraft. As usual, they reduced to non-Atlantean size again, changed their clothing and rushed upstairs to see Kenny and Jadeir. Kenny and Karin hugged while they talked to each other. Meanwhile, Sarah and Alyssia greeted Jadeir animatedly.

"I'm so glad to see you again, Karin. I don't want you going on another mission like this again," said Kenny.

"I'm sure there won't be any more now, because the star-ways are being much better monitored," replied Karin, "I expect you had quite a quiet time here, then?"

Kenny withdrew his arms from around Karin, and held her a little away from him so he could look into her eyes.

"Ah yes! We were all set for watching a few DVD's on the evening you left. Jadeir will tell you the story!"

They all sat round the kitchen table.

"We knew the characters who had bought your painting, Alyssia, had been taken back to Atlantis and dealt with there, so we didn't expect anything else. Jadeir heard a noise that night, downstairs in the shop at about 8pm, while we were sitting on the sofa having put a DVD in the slot," explained Kenny, "If we'd had the DVD on at the time, we'd never have heard it, and in fact, I didn't actually hear anything myself!"

"Extra sensory listening power, that's what I have!" exclaimed Jadeir, "I decided to turn invisible and then go and investigate. I went out at the back of the shop, and came round to the entrance. It was still locked, so I whizzed to the back entrance again and entered the shop. I sensed a presence in there, but didn't dare look at my crystal, as though it would have shown me exactly where the being was, it would have advertised my presence too. I just stopped by the door and listened. A sound came from within the shop beyond the counter, so I was about to move in that direction when I heard another sound in the gallery area.

The idea was to get them near each other, so I could tackle them both simultaneously. I concentrated on a small object on a stand that was non-breakable until it became dislodged and fell off, making a clattering sound. I could sense the beings turning in alarm and moving over to the source of disruption. I also caught a hint of a breath as one passed me. I followed him, and also heard a slight scuff of a shoe brushing the carpet. I speedily brought out the crystal and projected energy at both of them before they could draw breath. I heard the dull thud of their bodies collapsing on the floor. I phoned Kenny to tell him, and that I'd take them to Atlantis, but would return swiftly in case there were further repercussions."

"Go on! You're doing well," commented Kenny.

Jadeir mimed the action of sipping a cup of tea and so Sarah duly obliged.

"By the time they were taken to the temple in Chalidocea, their invisibility was wearing off," Jadeir continued, "and who do you think they were?" at this, Jadeir smiled knowingly, "one of them was the man who showed you your house, Sarah!"

Sarah looked at Jadeir in amazement.

"I can't believe all this attention to my house!" she replied, "but why were they prowling around the shop. Was there something specific they were looking for, or were they creating a red herring to confuse the issue, or covering for someone else's deeds elsewhere?"

"Yes Sarah, the latter I think," responded Jadeir, "and I stopped them in their tracks!"

"Who was the other person, Jadeir?" asked Alyssia.

"I don't know, we are still awaiting the answer from Chalidocea, and I think Sagario is helping the group of people involved, so he said he would let us know," replied Jadeir.

Sarah glanced at the table and noticed a letter addressed to her, and she picked it up.

"By the way, dear," asked Karin politely to Kenny, and she glanced at the oven.

"No sooner said than done, Karin!" cried Jadeir cheerfully.

A collection of food found its way onto the worktop, prepared itself, and was into a casserole dish, topped with water, stock and seasoning and into the oven in a matter of moments. Kenny shrugged his shoulders.

"You can't compete with that velocity of cooking power, can you!" he said.

"Great excuse dear!" laughed Karin.

"Hey everyone! I can move into my cottage now, the contract has gone through!" cried Sarah.

"Oh good, do you want to start moving in this weekend?" asked Alyssia.

"Yes! But I think I ought to check again if any of the rooms need painting first," replied Sarah, and she looked at everyone appealingly, "if so, I might need a team."

"I could round up the Pistyll Rhaeadr team!" cried Jadeir, "we're much quicker than humans."

"Go ahead and boast, we don't mind, as long as you would do the painting," said Kenny nonchalantly.

"No sooner said than done! You remember that phrase, don't you Kenny!" replied Jadeir, giving a pertinent stare, not unlike Kenny's expression.

"I certainly do!" responded Kenny, staring back, until they both began to laugh.

That weekend on the Saturday saw everyone over at Ty Bach Craig, except Kenny who was in the shop. The Pistyll Rhaeadr group, who consisted of Garalph, Leannah, Gadair and Kavanos, along with Jadeir, had painted the cottage walls in warm peaches and pinks, while Sarah was instructing Karin and Alyssia on how she would like to develop the garden. As for moving in, Sarah, Karin and Alyssia had found several items of furniture in an Oswestry saleroom the day before, and they had been delivered on the same day. Also, Sarah's friend in Cornwall, Geraldine, had arranged for Sarah's favourite furniture and items she had stored for her to be transported up within the next few days.

"Let's sort out the magic corner!" said Sarah; "I've been wanting to do this for ages!"

They each took an implement and wandered over to the group of trees, squeezed behind them, and began to clear the area.

"We'll need to connect the hose, or use a couple of buckets of water to clean up the well when we've finished," said Alyssia.

There were certainly plenty of tools left in that outhouse," remarked Karin.

"Yes indeed. I'm sure there's a hose included," responded Sarah.

"I'll go and have a look in a minute," replied Alyssia.

After a short while she went off to look. Jadeir and the Pistyll Rhaeadr group came to watch.

"We think a ceremony would be good to conduct, once that corner is cleared entirely," commented Jadeir.

"Well, I like the sound of that idea, thank you!" replied Sarah.

Alyssia returned with a hose, and found the water tap, attached it on, and unravelled it over to the trees.

"I'll go and switch it on, if one of you would like to grab the end," said Alyssia.

Sarah picked it up and Alyssia turned the tap on. The group of faces looking on swiftly multiplied as the well was cleaned up.

"Oh look! It has a fountain attachment too, that was just lying outside it. If it was cleaned up, it could be re-attached again," commented Sarah.

A stream of sunlight shone down, catching itself reflected in the well water, within the ceramic bowl, that had been inserted into the well's structure.

"The row of symbols prove to be the crown chakra right-brained images of the first four sets," said Alyssia.

"And the other three?" asked Sarah.

"Ah, I think, yes, they are the crown chakra left-brained images of set two to four," replied Alyssia.

"There seems to be something present at the base of the bowl, Sarah," said Alyssia.

"Oh yes, so there is," replied Sarah, "it's just a bit difficult to see under the dirt. I'll apply a bit more elbow grease to it!"

Sarah encouraged the Pistyll Rhaeadr group to help. Kavanos smiled sunnily and soon had the area sparkling clean.

"There are more symbols again under there," remarked Sarah.

"They look like base chakra symbols, a mixture from various sets up to number four, both left and right," explained Alyssia.

"Heaven and earth," said Jadeir, "they are linked together here, very healthy!"

"Absolutely!" cried the Pistyll Rhaeadr group.

"Is it a good time for that ceremony?" asked Sarah, "will it stop that red herring situation you mentioned Jadeir?"

"Oh yes, and it will!" replied Jadeir, "I intuit that Kenny has left Bertha in charge of the shop, and is almost here by now."

"All right," said Sarah, "we'll await his lordship and then start. Please make arrangements for the ceremony as you wish," she said to Jadeir and his friends.

The group formed into a circle around the well and trees, and asked the others to enter inside it, facing inwards towards the well at the south-western side of the garden. Kenny appeared at that moment and stepped briskly into the circle.

While the blessing progressed, Sarah felt as if she were back in her dream; the giant bowl around her, the voice murmuring that she did know about some of the codes now, but the real purpose of the well would still have to be understood. The others felt a difference too, and they would recall their experiences afterwards.

The Pistyll Rhaeadr group had blessed the well, and asked that it be used for spiritual purposes, and to be linked to Atlantis and the star-ways. They indicated for Sarah to add her piece to the ceremony. She walked right up to the well and stood half sideways, so the others could hear what she said.

"I bless this well too, and that the secrets of this place will be known and its full potential be revealed," she said.

A delicate perfume came into the air, and as people began to be aware of its presence, faint musical tones also could be heard. Everyone instinctively drew closer to the well, and they all began chanting something that Jadeir and his friends initiated. With that, the colours of the well area became brighter, and every object also became more clearly defined, and it was apparent that the area became radiant. Everyone gave thanks to god and goddess and withdrew from the well, while still facing it, to have a moment's reflection.

There was a sudden crackle of energy, an increase in light, and a familiar figure appeared by the well.

"Greetings everyone! I thought I'd try to get here and see the well for myself. Sorry I missed the ceremony!" smiled Hudlath.

He was wearing his Atlantean clothes, and stepped forwards to greet everyone.

"The new improved star-ways are making it easier to move around to all sorts of places!" he explained, and looked pointedly at everyone, "and do you not know yet of the origin of this well?"

They all looked at each other and back to Hudlath.

"The codes give it away?" asked Karin.

"But that information could have been taken from Atlantis and brought to this present time," suggested Alyssia.

"The well may go back to ancient times, but the information and the bowl could have been superimposed and used while the house was unoccupied," said Sarah.

Hudlath spun round to look at Sarah.

"Yes! You've concluded the situation, Sarah! But how did they get the information?" he stated.

"From Maraya when she was transmitting to Alyssia?" asked Karin.

"No, it was before that," answered Hudlath.

"Someone who knew the Atlantean temples?" questioned Alyssia.

"Were the cards extant in Atlantis at any time?" asked Sarah.

"The cards were in the temples, but hadn't been since the caskets' disappearance, which, of course was during the first break up of the continents, in one instance, and during the end times in the second. They were briefly re-united once or twice, and kept together in the mountain temple or at Chalidocea for up to fifty years at a time, before being stolen by the renegades when their communities set up in various places, usually on the surrounding islands to the continent. Their social structures were based on greed, power and the usual negative tendencies as you can imagine, and they would come over in hordes to the mainland to ambush and start skirmishes periodically," explained Hudlath.

"Was it so difficult to keep them at bay, Hudlath?" asked Kenny; "those heavily disguised used house salesmen renegades, I can imagine!" remarked Kenny.

"Those used house salesmen had an uncanny knack with dark magic and misuse of crystals, unfortunately, and they caused many problems and were tricky to tackle," answered Hudlath.

"Well, the fact that it is resolved is the main importance now!" remarked Sarah.

"Yes that is so, and it has been resolved," replied Hudlath, "but the fact was that renegades could enter any time period and cause havoc, the long overdue star-way design improvement has solved this problem once and for all. Partly overdue because there were so many other problems elsewhere in ours and other neighbouring universes."

"I hope you don't mind my asking about the other reason why it wasn't enacted before now, Hudlath?" asked Alyssia.

"That is worth bringing up!" replied Hudlath, "you see, we can't always take action until an action or set of actions, or even a will to make change takes place on Earth, or another planet; only then this acts as a catalyst for change elsewhere in the universe, which then resonates back to Earth etc., and creates the perfect environment for change."

"I see, Hudlath," replied Alyssia; "so it encourages us to understand things more effectively, and take responsibility."

"Indeed it does!" and Hudlath smiled, "and now everyone, would you like to see what Sarah's well can do?"

Everyone drew closer, all encircling the trees.

"I know you all have your crystals with you these days, so please bring them out," he announced.

With crystals in their hands, Hudlath said they were going to visit a place on the star-way to the Pleiades that is a viewing platform or link to greater star systems. Intrigued, they were quick to prepare.

"We are going to visit somewhere very beautiful, though you will be aware of still being here simultaneously, just follow what I say and do!" explained Hudlath, "I'm setting my crystal for a destination. All you have to do is ask your crystals to link into mine."

As they did so, Hudlath's figure began to grow fainter, and then everyone else followed suit. The rushing light of the star-way gave way to the beautiful planet of Pharon. They could see the new star-way that stretched past the Pylon of Phairos, but to where? Hudlath had not revealed its destination yet. They continued along this new star-way, going increasingly faster as they progressed. There was a blinding flash, then tremendous peace and stillness entered their minds. It almost made them gasp in amazement. After a moment's adjustment, they were aware of being watched by a group of tall figures they couldn't quite see, but waves of awesome love came to them all so powerfully, that they all smiled, felt very happy, but also moved at the same time. The figures greeted them kindly, and encouraged them to return again after a moment. Then they were all back in their bodies and adjusting to everyday reality.

"That was splendid, who were those lovely beings?" asked Sarah.

"I saw a lot of magenta, gold and mauve when I saw those beings," remarked Alyssia.

"I saw peaches and greens," commented Sarah.

"I only saw white," said Karin, "maybe you just see the soul colours you're drawn to, which are enhanced by such encounters."

"They were from Sirius!" replied Hudlath, "it was your reward for helping on the mission. You see, it is important to know that there are many intelligent forces at work to help the personal state through to universal state evolution, and it is in fact a natural occurrence, and if it was not to be the case, it would be like the solar system suddenly grinding to a halt, babies never growing up and seeds never becoming plants and trees. So, you can see that the symbiosis of it all, that highly evolved star systems helping those less evolved, because in time, they will progress further, and the less evolved ones will take their place in turn."

"That means we truly are on a threshold as we have been aware of for a while, that Earth and her inhabitants are progressing to a state of knowing, taking responsibility for themselves and their planet, and are ready to link to higher intelligence for real change," explained Hudlath.

"Will this link help to bring more Sirian energy to the Earth?" asked Sarah.

"It's certainly a beginning, indeed," replied Hudlath.

They wandered off to have some refreshments indoors, and were settled in the lounge, when the doorbell rang.

"That's funny, I wasn't expecting anyone!" cried Sarah.

"Time for a quick change!" exclaimed Hudlath.

His Atlantean clothes transformed into his green velvet jacket and green trousers. The Pistyll Rhaeadr group and Jadeir became invisible, while Sarah went to the door.

"Hello there! My name is Annie and I live in the house on the far side of the crossroads. I know you've got a group of people with you at present, so I won't bother you now! Here's a little gift to welcome you here."

"How kind," replied Sarah.

She looked into Annie's eyes. There was a strange poignancy that came to Sarah, as if she'd known Annie before, and she looked at Annie curiously.

"I'm sure I've known you before," remarked Sarah.

"Yes, in these parts, but some centuries ago!" replied Annie, self-assuredly.

"Won't you come in?" asked Sarah again, "everyone else is of the same mind."

Annie smiled, "well, I thought so, and I'd be delighted!"

"This is Annie everyone, an old friend from a past life!" announced Sarah.

Everyone laughed and welcomed Annie into the lounge.

"Open your present," encouraged Annie, as she found a space on the sofa, and then the Pistyll Rhaeadr group and Jadeir re-appeared as from another room.

Sarah carefully unwrapped the pink and gold covered gift to reveal a little ornament; it was a well with an elf and fairy next to it. A phrase was typed onto an adhesive label placed on the underside. Sarah read it out aloud.

"This well is a symbol of feminine energy, that is tended by the elemental spirits, and those who respect this, hold a key to unlocking the secrets of nature and life itself."

"How incredible!" cried Sarah, "did you know I have a natural well in the garden?"

"No I didn't, but something in me knew this was just the right thing to give you. I've only been in the house myself for a few weeks," replied Annie.

"What kind of work do you do?" asked Alyssia.

"I teach meditation and yoga, and am keen on self-sufficiency and growing your own food, that type of thing," she replied.

There were a lot of ideas exchanged about self-sufficiency, and Annie was fascinated by the elemental presence.

Eventually, Hudlath announced it was time for him to depart, and Jadeir and his friends got up to leave too. They left by the front door, so as not to startle Annie, promptly disappearing to their destinations once out of sight. Hudlath and Jadeir returned to Atlantis, and then Annie got up to leave.

"Do call round any time Annie!" said Sarah, "we may need your help in the garden!"

"I will, it will be a pleasure," she replied.

"Don't forget Annie, we would be happy to have you on board the good ship Plas Myrddin, if the room suits your purpose, just call in," said Kenny.

"I will," replied Annie, and then she departed.

"I suppose I should be looking for a flat myself as I've overstayed my welcome long enough, and my paintings are beginning to sell well," commented Alyssia.

"We don't mind you staying in our flat, Alyssia," said Kenny, "we like company."

"I've got enough room in my place for you to live here too, Alyssia," replied Sarah.

"What it is to be popular!" cried Alyssia, "well, that would be nice, to come and go wherever I felt I'd like to paint, as different environments do enhance inspiration! I shall be coming over to help in your garden too, Sarah."

"Returning to the subject of the well, I do feel that more significant experiences will happen with that well, and so we must be aware of that," remarked Sarah.

"There's a correlation between your life at the waterfall and this one isn't there?" asked Karin.

"My! So there is!" responded Sarah, "I will have to be more perceptive to the full potential of that, and what it is all leading towards."

"We'll all try our best to help in this," said Alyssia.

"By the way, Hudlath forgot to tell us about his jacket changing trick!" commented Kenny, "how do you think he does it?"

"Perhaps he's wearing both, and just doses them with withering plant, so one or other disappears accordingly," said Sarah.

"Go on!" replied Karin, curiously.

"I think the garments are made of etheric substance, which he just apports," explained Sarah.

"You could be right," said Kenny, "we don't have the skills to use matter in constructive, thoughtful ways to such a degree, but we can learn if we are willing and responsible, it is always possible."

"Yes, I'm sure it is so," replied Sarah.

We'll be over tomorrow," they said, "for more adventures!"

They all talked some more and then Kenny, Karin and Alyssia departed for Oswestry.

Sarah laughed and waved to them as they went over to Alyssia's car. Kenny and Karin then went over to their van and drove off. Sarah went back indoors and locked the front door. She took the mugs and plates from the occasional table through to the kitchen. Soft moonlight shone across the garden, alighting on the corner where the well was, under the trees. She felt drawn to go out there and so she went out the back door, walking softly over the damp grass. Faint musical tones could be heard and the air became scented again. Two lights appeared by the well as Sarah approached. One revealed itself as a fairy and the other as an elf.

"We are two of the guardians here, and watched your ceremony today," said the fairy.

"We know of your good intent and therefore we appeared to you. We were busy so couldn't join in. My name is Alendrin, and this is Miara," said the elf.

"Thank you, and I am very happy to have you in my garden," replied Sarah, "and who are the other guardians?"

"You will find out soon!" they replied cryptically.

They faded away, and so did the music and scented air. Sarah looked up at the moon a moment, and then returned to the house.

161

She did some unpacking in her bedroom, and then went to bed. Her dreams held tall figures all converging on her well vortex, and like the springtime growth that had re-awakened Atlantis in Anchorin's time, she sensed that the aftermath of that, and the new order of the star-ways would result in something similar in the present day.

Sarah awoke the next morning with a thought in her mind, as if prompted by her dreams.

'I must tell the others! We must begin writing a book about our experiences and share them with those who may be interested. I think it is important.'

She got up to look out of the window, which overlooked the well.

'There's something there in that well, how strange!' she thought.

She dressed quickly, ran downstairs and outside. What she'd seen upstairs was a strip of newspaper.

'I wonder whose rubbish this is?' she thought, and picked it up.

Something inspired her to read the strip of paper, so she took it into the kitchen and sat down. She could scarcely believe what she read.

'Plas Myrddin's latest selling point proved to be of great interest to a certain sector of the public. Their new trilogy about Atlantis talks of travels across time, rescuing caskets of spiritual value, and helping to redeem the cosmic order of life itself. Collaborated by four intriguing people, the public interest is ever growing stronger.'

An Overall View of the Trilogy

The Atlantean trilogy could be seen as a fantasy story, or one of those Merlin-like tales that abound. It was channelled to me as a tale that evokes much about life outside the everyday world that we know. Its purpose is evocative and to inspire.

It talks of ancient times when temples were regarded with deep respect, for the priests were the guardians of their world and mentors of the populace. They understood how to use energy to benefit people, and the planet. They respected the sacred nature of life, and many beings shared their world. Unicorns, Pegasus', benign beings from other planets, and elementals constantly worked with them, who would also give advice and wisdom to temples.

All this would have taken place predominantly in the golden ages of the Atlantean culture, and their clairsentience, especially in the priesthood and priestess hood, would have been well developed.

This psychic power became so degenerated during the last kali ages at the end times of Atlantis, that a lot of gifts they had then, were abused, causing a lot of potency to be shut down. This, of course is why so much has been coming to light spiritually in recent times.

I have tried to show the contrasts between times periods, and how their use of technology is echoed in our present culture. At best, it was used with discrimination for their work and with spiritual intent, unlike the end times, when it was extensively used with materialistic intent, like today, to control the public.

In book 1, the clairsentient abilities becomes awakened in the people who enter the story and they travel to Atlantis to help find the caskets and bring that lost potency back into life.

In book 2, the Atlantean Codes enter the story, first brought to Atlantis from the Pleiades, but lost in time. They, like the caskets, have transformative powers and bring light to restore harmony along the star-ways, and for self-transformation.

Book 3 links the Garden of Eden on Earth to two other planets, Lemuria, the spirit world, and the centre of Earth. It aims to resolve and restore harmony on Earth, the Oswestry group bring back their wisdom from these places, including a visit into future times, and then give their insights to others.

All in all, the trilogy intends to show what wisdom these ancient civilisations had, another version of the age-old wisdom to bring inspiration.

Like the lady who wrote a number of books on ancient wisdom, Dion Fortune, some were fiction to evoke wisdom from an intuitive right-brained angle, and others were factual, to bring through information for the left brained side.

I think both story and factual information had equal validity, since, we don't always know everything that happened in ancient cultures, and so a bit of intuitive insightfulness can bring through information that wouldn't be possibly available via the intellect.

www.ingramcontent.com/pod-product-compliance
Lightning Source LLC
Chambersburg PA
CBHW051242170626
46809CB00004B/1445